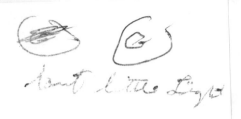

Love is
a time of enchantment:
in it all days are fair and all fields
green. Youth is blest by it,
old age made benign:
the eyes of love see
roses blooming in December,
and sunshine through rain. Verily
is the time of true-love
a time of enchantment — and
Oh! how eager is woman
to be bewitched!

UNTIL WE MEET AGAIN

What was life all about anyway? Other girls fell in love, were loved in return, married, had children — achieved normal happiness. Twice the wizard curtains had opened for her, revealing a bright, promising life ahead, and twice they had been cruelly jerked shut, condemning her to hopeless rejection. It had taken her a long time to recover from the first blow. Would she ever recover from this one?

ANN FARRINGTON

UNTIL WE MEET AGAIN

Complete and Unabridged

ULVERSCROFT
Leicester

First published in the
United States of America

First Large Print Edition
published October 1993

British Library CIP Data

Farrington, Ann
    Until we meet again.—Large print ed.—
Ulverscroft large print series: romance
I. Title
823 [F]

ISBN 0–7089–2951–6

Published by
F. A. Thorpe (Publishing) Ltd.
Anstey, Leicestershire

Set by Words & Graphics Ltd.
Anstey, Leicestershire
Printed and bound in Great Britain by
T. J. Press (Padstow) Ltd., Padstow, Cornwall

This book is printed on acid-free paper

1

BETTY LANE'S large brown eyes were filled with fear and uncertainty as the jumbo jet streaked westward across the Pacific towards Hawaii. She could not shake a nagging doubt about the future. Was she doing the right thing — running away to a new job in an unfamiliar corner of the world? 'A change of scenery won't get you over the disappointment of a one-sided love affair. That's got to come from within you,' her good friend, Peg Waters, had advised. Peg was right. Betty knew that. Yet, remaining in St. Louis had been of no help. Surely new surroundings would offer some sort of relief from her heartache.

As the aircraft slowed late that afternoon, preparatory to landing, a hostess in a bright orange and blue muu muu came along the aisle, checking to make sure each passenger's seat belt was fastened. She smiled at Betty.

"Have you enjoyed the flight?" she asked.

The hostess had made a point of speaking to the small, well-built blonde twice during the trip, for she had noticed her look of apprehension when she came aboard in Los Angeles. She had mistaken it for a fear of flying.

"Yes," Betty nodded and managed a weak smile.

Through the plane's window, Betty could see nothing but white clouds and a grayish blue ocean. Then, all at once, the jet made a turn and spectacular lime green mountains came into view. What she guessed was Pearl Harbor, that tragic spot in history, came next as the plane went into a long glide. A smooth landing, followed by the reverse thrust of the engines, reduced the aircraft's forward speed on the runway. Several minutes later, it taxied up to the unloading ramp and the engines were turned off. Immediately the passengers began filling the aisle and gathering their belongings.

Betty stepped out of the plane into a bright summer afternoon. She was amazed and pleased with the change from the cold, bleak winter morning she had left behind in St. Louis. The warm sun felt good bearing down on her head and shoulders. As a small motor train took her and the other passengers to the main terminal building she caught her first glimpse of tall Royal palm trees swaying gently in the trade winds.

Suddenly a magic moment came over her, as if adventure and romance beckoned just beyond those palms. But the feeling quickly passed as she stood alone and forlorn in the milling crowd around the baggage carousels. Many of the passengers were being greeted and presented with fragrant and colorful carnation leis. Islanders in gaudy aloha shirts and dresses cried a joyous welcome to arriving friends and relatives. Betty could not help feeling a bit wistful, but at the same time she enjoyed the colorful scene.

"Need a taxi, Miss?" asked a porter.

"Yes, please," she looked around gratefully.

"Where to?" he asked.

She gave him the name of a hotel at

Waikiki where she was supposed to have reservations.

"Let me have your baggage stubs. I'll take your bags right out there." He pointed to a limousine and waved at the driver.

Betty went out to the car where the driver was already holding the door open for her, as if she were an heiress and he a private chauffeur.

"Aloha," he said, to Betty's amusement and delight.

"Aloha," she replied experimentally. It was the first time she had used the word in conversation.

A few minutes later, she was riding regally alone in the back seat of the limousine, her head swivelling from one side to the other as they went toward Honolulu on Nimitz Highway. The piquant odor from the pineapple canneries filled the air as they drove through a factory and warehouse district. They passed the busy Honolulu docks, where the salt air mingled with the odor of tar and oil, and skirted the downtown financial district of Honolulu. From there they were suddenly on a wide boulevard that the driver, after learning that this was Betty's first visit to the Islands, said was the Ala Moana, a name that meant nothing to Betty.

Across a small bridge, they made a sweeping turn among beautiful high rise apartment buildings. At another turn she saw a street sign that said Kalakaua, which she recognized as the street where her hotel was located. On her right was Fort DeRussey. Then, five minutes later, they turned into a short narrow street, made a swing around a circular drive, amid a profusion of tropical trees and flowers, and stopped under a porte-cochere. An immaculate doorman in a pink blazer, white trousers and white shoes, helped her out of the limousine and welcomed her as if she owned the place. The driver got out, came around and told her the tab which was nine dollars and sixty cents.

Betty blinked. She was brought down to earth with a thud by the charge. She paid it, but made up her mind right then never to get into another taxi in Hawaii. There were already enough ways to go bankrupt.

Up six wide, red-carpeted steps she went through an entrance without doors into a gorgeous lobby. A pretty Filipino girl smiled from behind the registration desk and asked if she had a reservation.

"Yes. I hope so. My name is Betty Lane."

Her former boss, Mr. George Placer, president of the Placer Public Relations Agency back in St. Louis, had said he could make the reservation for her, even though the hotels along Waikiki were usually booked solid this time of year. She hoped he had been successful.

The girl looked through a large file and nodded. "Here you are. Room three-six-five. Sign this card please and here is your key. Take the elevator over there to the third floor. Your bags will come right up."

Betty went to the third floor and there, prophetically, lost her way for the first time in Hawaii. After two wrong turns, she was directed by one of the maids and finally found the room around a corner near the end of a long hallway. The porter was already there with her luggage. She handed him a tip.

"Enjoy you stay with us," said the small Oriental man as he pulled the louvered door shut behind him.

Betty looked around the room. It was beautifully decorated, large and spacious with the highest ceiling she had ever seen in a room. She went to the window and looked out. Below was the famous beach at Waikiki. Diamond Head, that huge brooding Sphinx-like extinct volcano, was just beyond. And everything overlooked the deep blue swelling waters of the Pacific. She felt like clapping her hands with pleasure at the sight of surfboards and outrigger canoes skimming toward the beach on the forward slope of on-rushing waves.

But, she reminded herself, this was no time to be admiring the scenery. She was supposed to report for work at nine o'clock in the morning at Benning & Associates, Public Relations Agency, a firm that had connections with Mr. Placer back in St. Louis. She was to serve as secretary to Mr. Benning, whom she did not know, for a period of two years.

After a shower she changed to a light dress and went down to the lobby. She was not hungry, for on the plane she had eaten beef terriyaki braised and garnished with a slice of pineapple. But she thought a snack might be advisable before going to bed. Besides she needed direction as to how she could get to Benning & Associates in the morning.

"How do I get to Kapiolani and Keeaumoko streets?" she asked the Bell Captain. Betty had been told that the Benning Agency was located in a building on the corner of that intersection. She had trouble pronouncing the Hawaiian names and it took a second try before the Bell Captain, a small Japanese man, understood what she was saying.

"You go to Kuhio. Dat's where da busses run," he said.

"Where is Kuhio?"

"Next street beyond Kalakaua. You see signs of da bus stops. Wait dere."

Betty thanked him, then asked where she might get something to eat. He pointed down the lobby. She followed his direction and ended up in a large, somewhat formal restaurant that over-looked the ocean. The lightest thing on the menu was a Manoa lettuce salad

8

that turned out to be twice as much as she wanted. But she enjoyed watching the sunset and lighting of the torches. Presently her practiced musical ear heard Hawaiian music. She looked around. A trio of singers accompanying themselves with a ukulele, guitar and bass were standing on a low platform at one end of a small dance floor. Altogether it was a satisfying evening for Betty. When she returned to her room she went to sleep almost the moment her head was on the pillow.

The next morning she awoke refreshed, ready to begin her job. After a breakfast of papaya — the first she had ever tasted — blueberry muffins and coffee, she found her way over to Kuhio, spotted a bus stop and waited in a large crowd of people. When the bus arrived the crowd surged forward and Betty was propelled into the bus where she told the bus driver to let her off at Kapiolani.

"We don't go there," he said.

"But they told me at the hotel — "

"Sorry. This bus goes to the Ala Moana shopping center then comes back to Waikiki."

"Oh dear — "

"Where do you want to go?"

"To Kapiolani and Keeaumoko."

"Okay. Stay on this bus. Get off at the center. Then go *mauka*." And with that the driver closed the door, sang out for everyone to move back in the bus and took off.

Fifteen minutes later, after packing in more passengers at other bus stops, the driver announced that they were arriving at the center. He added that he hoped everyone had brought along plenty of money, because there was much to buy at Ala Moana.

Betty got out along with the other passengers. She did not know what the driver had meant by going *mauka* — going toward the mountains — but she really couldn't go any other way for across the boulevard was a park and beyond that the Pacific Ocean. She followed the other passengers, through a giant car-filled parking space, to the shopping center.

No one had prepared her for what she got into. It was, a sign said, the largest shopping center in the world. She believed it. She kept walking, among a myriad of shops, looking for Kapiolani. Finally she stopped and asked a security guard.

"It's that way," he gestured.

Betty followed his direction and came out on another vast parking lot. She was getting worried. The time was going faster than she had thought. It was already nine o'clock and she was supposed to be in Mr. Benning's office by now. She stopped to ask another security guard.

"You go out this parking lot and across Kona. Go north to the first street you come to. That's Kapiolani, the one you want."

Betty started out with a sinking feeling. She glanced at her watch. It was now ten after nine. This was no way to start off with a new boss. She walked rapidly and finally found Kapiolani. Now which way, she wondered. She asked a passer by. He did not know. He was a stranger here himself. Desperately, she moved along the street, looking and wondering. Finally, she stopped a native girl and asked again. This time she got some help.

Keeaumoko? It's back that way, one block."

Betty looked around. She saw the intersection and also a tall office building which she could not understand how she had missed. She had been going in the opposite direction.

"Thanks a million," she said and hurried off.

She almost ran back to the building. Inside she found a directory, took the elevator to the sixth floor and arrived at Benning & Associates almost totally out of breath. She went in.

"Mr. Benning's office?" she asked a Chinese girl at a nearby desk.

It was a larger operation than Mr. Placer's. She saw two men seated at desks, beyond the girl. The girl motioned toward a door marked private.

"I'll bet you're Miss Lane from St. Louis," said the girl.

"Yes."

"Welcome to Hawaii."

"Thanks. Is Mr. Benning in?"

"Yes, and I imagine he's waiting to meet you."

Betty hurried to the door marked

private and knocked. An authoritative masculine voice within told her to enter. Betty opened the door.

She stared at the young man who sat behind a large executive desk. He was tall, broad shouldered, deeply tanned and wearing a white suit, solid white tie on a brown shirt and a matching brown handkerchief in the breast pocket. His jaw was firm and his smooth shaven face was well proportioned. His hair was black and had a slight wave. He was so handsome that Betty was momentarily at a loss for words.

"Mr. Benning?" she finally managed.

"Yes." His voice was deep and resonant.

"I'm Betty Lane."

"I thought you were."

He looked her over intently, his dark eyes taking in every detail of her, from her blonde head, short nose and wide mouth to her well rounded calves and slim ankles. She felt a strange and embarrassing excitement as she stood on the beige carpeting undergoing his scrutiny. She thought she saw a spark of approval in his eyes and a faint smile on his lips. But that notion was shattered as

13

he addressed her sharply.

"You're late!"

"I — " she was taken aback by his reprimand. "I'm sorry but I got lost and — "

"Never mind. You're finally here. Your desk is right outside the door. I put some rough copy news releases on your desk. Please type them at once, then make a dozen copies each on the duplicator."

Betty retreated through the door and closed it behind her. She went to the desk and sat down. Her knees were weak. She was grateful for a chance to be resting in a chair. The girl who had greeted her when she first arrived came over.

"My name is Audrey Ching. And these two are Billy Everett and Warson Graham," she said pleasantly.

The two men came over and shook hands with Betty. Everett was a small man with a dark mustache and horn-rimmed glasses, probably in his early twenties. Graham was older, rather gaunt and with evasive blue eyes. They both welcomed her to the Islands and to Benning & Associates.

"Are you the Associates?" Betty asked.

14

"I guess you could call us that," Billy Everett laughed. "But you should also include Audrey and now yourself. So again, welcome aboard." They went back to their desks, but Audrey lingered.

"Let me know if I can help. I do stenographic work for those two. Jack likes to keep his secretary, who was Jane Kimura and now you, free for his own work."

Betty was surprised to hear the girl refer to Mr. Benning as Jack. He sure didn't act like anyone who would be on such familiar terms with the help. Betty had been in his office less than a minute and she was already terrified of him.

She wondered how Jane Kimura had gotten along with him. It was because of her that Betty was here.

A month ago Benning had informed Mr. Placer by letter that his secretary was moving to St. Louis. The girl's husband would be attending Washington University dental school and she needed work to help out while he was getting his degree. Could the Placer Public Relations Agency help her find a job?

Mr. Placer, a kind and understanding

15

man, knew that Betty had been unhappy because of a broken engagement and thought it might be good for her to have a change of scenery. It had been he who had suggested she change jobs with Mrs. Kimura for a year or two, providing, of course, that it was agreeable with Benning. A long distance call to Hawaii had determined that it would be.

So here Betty was, wondering more than ever if she had done the right thing.

"He told me to start typing some releases, so I'd better get busy," she said. Audrey went back to her own desk.

Betty found the releases in the incoming box. She got out paper and a carbon, twisted them into the typewriter and went to work. Concentrating on typing might help quiet the nerves that Mr. Benning had set jangling.

"Please get me the Mayor on the phone."

It was Benning's voice coming suddenly from a small intercom box on her desk. Betty was so startled that she jumped, hitting two wrong keys on the typewriter. Frantically she looked around for a phone book. Audrey hurried over.

"Jane kept a book of important telephone numbers in the desk. I think it's in this drawer." She opened it and took out a large, loose-leaf folder. "Here it is."

Betty picked up the phone and dialed. To her surprise a man's voice came on saying, "Mayor's office."

"Mr. Benning is calling. May he speak with the Mayor?" Betty looked at the Mayor's name. She couldn't come close to pronouncing it. So she handled it the only way she knew how.

"One moment."

The voice faded from the phone and a minute later another man's voice came on.

"Yes, Jack. What can I do for you?"

"I — I'm sorry," Betty stammered. "One moment, please, your Honor. I'll get Mr. Benning on the wire."

She searched frantically for a buzzer that would alert Mr. Benning to the call. She pressed the first button she found, for a confused instant, she and the Mayor and Benning were all on the phone — Betty telling her boss that the

Mayor was waiting; the Mayor saying "hello, Jack," and Benning shouting at Betty to get off the line. Betty hung up and groaned.

Her new boss was making a nervous wreck out of her. She had not been here long enough to know her way around her own desk. Yet, here he was, expecting a great performance from her! She was beginning to resent such treatment. He could at least give her an hour or so to get acclimated, she thought. She looked around. The men paid no attention to her, being absorbed in their own work. But Audrey smiled in her direction.

"You'll get used to him," she said.

Perhaps she would, Betty thought. She had never known a man who came on so strong. But, given time, maybe she could cope with his habits and idiosyncrasies. Adjusting to a boss's moods was done every day in the business world. It was the impact of his physical appearance that had upset her the most. He disturbed her in a frightening way.

"I wonder," said Betty helplessly and went back to her typing.

2

BETTY finished her typing and spent the remainder of the morning getting oriented around the office. She was grateful for the time because she needed to familiarize herself with the Agency's clients. Such knowledge was important to a secretary so she could perform her duties efficiently. The list of clients was impressive.

It consisted of the Iwalani Shipping Company, the Mid-Pacific Bank and Trust, the Island Land and Development Company, the Kaimana Car Leasing Company, the Ke'ala of Hawaii flowers exporting business and, last but by no means least, the Kokusai Denki Corporation of Japan. Benning & Associates was a viable enterprise, thanks, no doubt, to its dynamic president.

The only account with which Betty was already familiar, at least in a small way, was Kokusai Denki. Mr. Placer, back

19

in St. Louis, had handled some mid-west work for Benning & Associates in connection with the Japanese firm. It was a company that specialized in electronics but it also had heavy investments abroad, many in the United States.

By noon, just as Betty began to feel reasonably calmed down, Benning burst out of his office.

"I'll be at lunch until two o'clock, in case anyone calls. If it's urgent you can reach me at the Club."

And, without even telling her where or what the Club was, he disappeared into the hall, heading for the elevator.

"Whew, is he always this wound up?" Betty asked Audrey.

"This is one of his calmer days. Do you want to go to lunch? You and I are supposed to take turns staying here to answer the phones."

"Maybe I'd better. Is there a place in this building?"

There was. Audrey gave her directions. Betty ate a sandwich and drank a cup of coffee at a small sandwich shop. She was back in the office in half an hour.

"You could have stayed longer," said

Audrey, surprised at seeing her back so soon.

"No. I still have a lot to learn right around the office. Find out what I still need to know. Why don't you go now?"

"Okay, but I won't be back. Jack gave me the afternoon off. My sister is getting married next week and wants me to help with some bridal arrangements," said the Chinese girl.

"Well, I guess any boss who would do that for an employee can't be all bad," Betty observed.

"You'll like him better as you get to know him," Audrey assured her.

Everett and Graham had left together to work on a project for the Island Land and Development Company. They, too, would be gone for the remainder of the day. So Betty made the best of her time alone. The phone rang only once.

"Benning & Associates," said Betty, lifting the receiver.

"Let me speak to Jack," came a girl's voice that had the ring of imperious authority.

"I'm sorry, but Mr. Benning is not here. He will be back at two o'clock.

Who shall I say called?"

"Cheryl." With that the girl hung up.

Betty shrugged and put down the receiver. If the girl had been patient for another two seconds Betty could have told her where Benning could be reached, at the Honolulu Press Club. It was the one he had referred to as 'the Club,' when he left the office. Audrey had filled Betty in on that.

Benning was back at two, as he had said he would be. She gave him the message from the girl. He nodded, said nothing and went into his office. After a bit, he called to her.

"Can you come in, please, and bring your steno book."

She entered his office, vowing to do her work well. Betty sat down beside his desk and mounted one knee upon the other. She held her pad and pencil poised. Benning eyed her shapely legs for a second, then quickly dictated a short news release for the society section of the papers. It had to do with a Miss Cheryl Canton and a party that she was giving for a Captain and Mrs. Henry Marsh, whom the Navy was transferring to an assignment back on the mainland.

When Betty had it typed up she took it back in and put it on his desk. She started out again, but he told her to remain while he read it.

"It's okay. Now take it to Cheryl and have her look it over. She lives in Kahala, not far from the Hilton. It's on the beach side between Hunakai and Kealaolu. I forget the exact address, but you can find it. Tell her I'm tied up."

Betty nodded and started out again.

"Wait. You'll have to take my car. It's down in the parking space. A white Thunderbird with red interior. You can't miss it." He tossed her the keys.

This time when she left, he did not call her back. She found the Canton home address in the telephone directory and wrote it down. The Hawaiian street names that Benning had rattled off so easily left Betty entirely confused. She had no idea where Kahala was. For that matter, she had no idea where the parking lot was. But this time she resolved to make sure where she was going and how to get there before starting off.

On the main floor, she asked a building attendant how to get to both the parking lot and the Kahala address. Showing her the parking lot was easy.

"But Kahala is on the other side of Diamond Head," he said. "The quickest way to get there is on the Freeway."

"And how do I get to that?" she asked. "I've never driven around here and I don't know the street names at all. I've only been here one day and know nothing about Honolulu," she confessed.

"Miss," he grinned, "you've got a problem. What you really need is a guide. But follow these directions and you won't go wrong." Then, obligingly, he wrote out a complete set of directions for her.

Betty was not sure that she would not go wrong. Her first obstacle was the Thunderbird. She had not driven a car for months, since selling her father's car after he died. And she had never driven one as large as Benning's. Even with the seat pushed up her toe barely touched the brake and accelerator pedals. She had trouble getting it started, being unfamiliar with the many gadgets on the dashboard. But, finally, she made it. She pulled out into the traffic on Kapiolani Boulevard. All at once she was terrified. She gripped the steering wheel so hard that her knuckles turned white.

Following the directions as best she could, she drove out Kapiolani and eventually found the Freeway. The man had neglected to tell her that it was elevated and it took some extra driving to get up on it. Getting off at the correct exit was even more difficult. By the time she made it, she was worn out with anxiety. The directions were confusing. And the complicated Hawaiian names really bugged her. But in time, and after stopping twice to inquire, she finally found the entrance to the palatial Canton residence. She drove in a circular drive and parked in front of a large redwood door.

"I came to see Miss Canton. Where can I find her?" she asked of a Japanese gardener who was working on a high hedge. All around were enormous ginger blossoms, bird-of-paradise and exotic flowers that Betty had never seen before.

25

"You ring da bell at da door," said the gardener.

Betty went to the door. The home was quite modern with a low hanging green roof and large screened windows that looked out over a lovely tropical landscape. A huge butler in a white coat responded to her ring.

"May I see Miss Canton, please?"

"Who is calling?" the butler looked her over suspiciously.

"My name is Betty Lane." She wondered if the butler had been a wrestler, he was so big.

"And what is the nature of your visit?"

"I'm here to deliver a news release to Miss Canton for her approval," Betty told him, wondering why all the security precautions.

"Wait here," the man said.

"And tell her Mr. Benning sent me," Betty added.

The butler turned away, but at Betty's last remark he came back.

"In that event, please follow me."

He led Betty through a wide hall filled with works of Oriental and Polynesian art. They emerged on the other side of the house, onto a wide lanai that looked out over the most beautiful blue ocean Betty could ever imagine. He turned right and she followed him to a large swimming pool.

"A Miss Lane to see you," the butler announced.

Betty stared as a girl in a string bikini looked around from a lounge where she was reclining. On a marble topped table by her side was a tall, iced mint julep. She was a brunette with unblemished skin that was a deep brown from the Hawaiian sun. Betty could not see her eyes because she wore large sun glasses. But there was no mistaking her appearance. She was voluptuous and utterly gorgeous.

"What do you want?" asked the girl in the same imperious tone that Betty remembered hearing on the telephone.

"Mr. Benning sent this for you to look over." Betty took the news release out of a brown envelope and handed it to the girl.

"Why didn't Jack bring it himself?" she demanded.

"He said to tell you that he was tied up."

"Oh, he did, did he!" she said angrily. And with that she stood up and paced to the edge of the pool and back. She was considerably taller than Betty.

Cheryl Canton pursed her red lips and was silent. She did not even look at Betty who had the distinct notion that the girl had been more interested in seeing Jack Benning than in seeing the news release. She still had not looked at it.

"Next time he had jolly well better get out here in person," said the girl.

Betty did not know what to say to that. She stood there waiting. The girl had not invited her to sit down. Suddenly she was aware that the girl's eyes were on her.

"Who did you say you are?"

"I'm Betty Lane, Mr. Benning's secretary."

Cheryl Canton looked Betty over closely, then said, "I heard Jane Kimura was leaving. Why did Jack hire *you*?"

"She went to St. Louis with her husband. She's going to take the job I had back there and I'm replacing her out here."

"Why didn't Jack tell me?" she said with emphasis on the 'me.'

"I'm sure I don't know." Betty gestured helplessly. She was beginning not to like this girl. "Did you wish to make any changes in the release?"

"No. Why should I?" The brunette barely glanced at it then threw it back at Betty, who put it in the envelope and stood there waiting and wondering what she should do. The girl sat down on the lounge, stretched out her legs and took a long pull on her glass of mint julep.

Betty did not know how to answer the girl's question. She looked at Cheryl Canton nonplussed.

"Well, is there anything else you want?" asked the girl impatiently.

"No. I guess not."

"Then you may go." The brunette ordered.

Something in the tone and the words, all at once, brought Betty to rebellion. Her nerves had been rubbed raw over a period of time. She had contained her pent-up feeling behind a shield of pride and pretense. And today, from the time she had left the hotel this morning, she had met with one frustration after another. Moreover, her boss had added to her turmoil by barking orders at her. And now this haughty, nearly naked brunette, who, obviously, had all the good things in life that a person could want, was treating her like dirt.

"Gladly!" Betty shot back.

She whirled and marched out followed by Cheryl Canton's hateful glance. Betty got into the car. With a roar of the engine she shot out of the driveway onto the street. She was still boiling, inside, as she started back to the office. But the directions she had were only one way. She tried to remember how she had come.

Fifteen minutes later Betty was hopelessly lost on streets that were up and down like a roller coaster. Again, she asked directions by stopping and calling to a man on the sidewalk. He gestured and spoke in such broken English that he was no help at all. She drove on.

The notion that Benning expected her back within a reasonable length of time made her more nervous than ever. At one point she snarled up traffic at an intersection before getting headed again in what she hoped was the right direction. Tight-lipped, she drove along a street toward what appeared to be the Freeway, when suddenly a car loomed ahead. It was coming right at her.

Surprise and horror leaped into Betty's eyes. She gave a mighty yank on the wheel. She missed the car by inches but went over the curb. The crash that followed sent shock waves through every bone in her body. The next instant, a geyser of water arose from a shattered fire hydrant beside the car and cascaded, like a giant fountain, down on the roof.

Betty jumped out. Instantly she was soaked to the skin. She stood dripping, in the midst of a rapidly growing crowd, at the scene of the accident. The wail of an approaching siren assailed her ears and a police car screeched to a halt. Two officers jumped out. One ordered the crowd back. The other came over to Betty.

"What's going on here?" he asked, staring at the spurting fire hydrant. "Did you cause this?"

"I'm afraid so, officer," said Betty, trembling all of a sudden.

The policeman looked at her, but just then a fire department truck arrived and he had to clear the way. A news photographer pushed through the crowd and began taking pictures. The firemen pulled the Thunderbird, which had sustained considerable damage to the radiator and front grill, away from the water spout. They turned off the main and the fountain subsided.

"How did this happen, young lady?" asked one of the police officers.

"I swerved to avoid hitting another car," she admitted.

"Didn't you know you were on a one-way street, going in the wrong direction?"

"No," she said in a small contrite voice. Worse and more of it, she thought.

The final blow came when he asked for her driver's license. All at once, it dawned on her that she had not brought it with her to Hawaii. She had no occasion to carry the license for some time.

"I'm afraid I haven't got it with me."

"Where is it?"

"In St. Louis."

"Then you're not too far from home."

"Betty looked at him mystified. "Not too far?"

"Where is your home, Miss?"

"I just told you. In St. Louis."

"Oh! You mean St. Louis, Missouri," the officer exclaimed after a puzzled moment. "I thought you meant St. Louis Heights, right over that way. Well, this presents more of a problem. I'm afraid, I'll have to ask you to come to the station. Along with everything else, this involves destruction of city property."

"Then let's go," she said starting toward the police car. She was tired of being stared at by the crowd of people that surrounded the scene.

She got into the back seat of the police car and waited while one of the officers made note of the license plate on the Thunderbird. On the way, Betty recalled, with a mirthless smile, the workings of Murphy's Law — if there is a possibility of anything going wrong, it will. She wished she had never left St. Louis.

"What's this all about?" asked the desk sergeant when Betty stood before him at the police station. He stared at her soaked clothes.

"She hit a fire hydrant and busted it off," said the officer who stood beside her.

"Your name, please, Miss?" asked the sergeant.

"Betty Lane."

"And your address?"

"I'm from St. Louis, but at the moment I'm staying at the Royal Hawaiian Hotel."

"The officer said you did not have a driver's license."

"I've got one but it's back in St. Louis somewhere."

"Is the Thunderbird yours?"

"No."

"Oh, it's a rental then."

"No, sir. It belongs to my boss."

The officer looked confused. "Is he staying at the Royal too?"

"No. My boss is Mr. Jack Benning of the Benning & Associates Public Relations Agency here. I just started work there this morning."

"Were you driving with his permission?"

"Yes. He sent me on an errand."

"Surprise on him," said the sergeant dryly. "Somebody is liable for that fire

34

plug. Whether it's you or the owner of the car remains a matter between you and him. Then there is the matter of driving the wrong way on a one-way street. And, of course, driving without a license. Those are the charges against you."

"I'm guilty," Betty admitted abjectly.

"Don't you think you had better call someone? Your boss, maybe? At least he has a right to know about his car. If he doesn't get it off the street, we'll have it towed away."

Betty felt as if she were being swept along by events far beyond her ability to control. It had been in the back of her mind that she would have to let Mr. Benning know about this sooner or later. She guessed the sooner the better. She asked to use the phone.

When she heard her boss's voice on the line she spoke so softly he could hardly hear her.

"Who did you say it was?" he asked.

"Me. Betty Lane."

"Where the devil have you been? You should have been back an hour ago!"

"I know, but something happened that

could not be helped."

"Where are you?"

"At the police station."

"The police station!" he shouted. "What are you doing there?"

"Mr. Benning," she cried, breaking into tears. "I'm sorry, but could you come over here and help me?"

There was a long pause at the other end.

"Okay. I'll be right over. Is my car downstairs?"

"No. That's just one of the many problems."

3

"**W**HAT are you, a one-woman earthquake?" Jack Benning shook his head with disbelief as he and Betty stood by the wrecked Thunderbird examining the damage.

He had gotten a car from the leasing agency and had come to the police station where, after being informed of the charges against her and liability for the fire plug, he had made a call to City Hall and had her released on her own recognizance. She was to have her driver's license sent out from St. Louis and then appear in court at a later date. She and Benning had then driven to the scene of the accident.

"I'll pay for it. It was all my fault. I feel so badly about wrecking your car," she said contritely.

"Look. It's not my car. It belongs to the leasing agency. I rent it from them and they have insurance. Don't get the idea that I approve of what you did, but quit worrying about it. Now this," he looked at the broken fire hydrant, "is another matter."

"I know."

"I don't know how much these things cost, but I'm afraid you're liable, unless the insurance on the Thunderbird covers such contingencies. They're looking into it for us."

At that moment a tow truck arrived. Benning had made arrangements for the leasing company to have the Thunderbird picked up and taken to a garage.

"Somebody sure gave this a good jolt," the truck driver commented as he examined the caved in front portion of the Thunderbird. "How did it happen?"

"Ask the Princess Pupule. She was driving," said Benning, gesturing toward Betty.

"I was in the wrong. I didn't know this was a one-way street," she said. Her voice was so quiet that it was hard to hear. Tears had been just under the surface for an hour.

"There's nothing more we can do and it's too late to go back to the office. Come on, I'll drive you to the hotel," said Benning.

"You don't have to do that. I — "

"How the hell do you think you can get there on your own?" he interrupted.

Betty didn't know. She didn't know anything. She was in such an abysmal frame of mind that she wished she could blank out and come to at some later date. Leaving St. Louis had been a terrible mistake. She could not handle her problems out here in Hawaii, where everything and everybody were strange beyond belief. These people seemed to know how to live and cope. She had been a miserable failure in both departments.

He took her arm and propelled her to the car. There was nothing for her to do but get in. He went around and got behind the wheel.

"You shouldn't be taking the time to do this for me," she said.

"Shut up! I've got to go to the hotel anyway. I'm having a reception there in a few days and have to make some arrangements."

Betty said no more. At the hotel he gave the car to an attendant and they went in. She began to thank him, but was cut off.

"Go up to your room and get out of those soggy clothes. Then come back down. I'll be out around the Mai Tai bar."

"Yes, sir," she said meekly.

Betty could not imagine what he wanted with her at this late hour in the afternoon. She could have understood it better if he had said he never wanted to see her again. But she went to her room, removed her damp clothes and took a quick shower. After fixing her face and hair as best she could on such short notice, she put on a white dress with a red polka dot scarf, then went down to the Mai Tai bar on the ocean lawn of the hotel.

Benning was seated at a table between the bar and the Surf Room restaurant talking with an arresting Eurasian girl in a long red and gold brocade gown that was slit up one side to her thigh. A high stiff collar around her neck completed the Oriental garment. Her black hair was done in a beautiful high coiffure and on one side she wore an arrangement of lovely cymbidium orchids. Benning waved Betty over to the table.

When Betty arrived he stood up, put a fragrant plumeria lei around her neck and, to her utter astonishment, kissed her.

"Aloha and welcome to the Island," he smiled.

Betty suddenly felt light headed. The touch of his warm lips on hers made her tingle all over. She looked down at the lei. When she lifted her eyes they were covered with mist. His eyes were soft, looking back at her. How, she wondered, could he be so rough on her only a few minutes ago and now so thoughtful and tender?

"Thanks," she stammered. "Gee, thanks a million!"

"I thought you might be needing a bit of aloha after what you've been through today. And, besides, it's an old Hawaiian custom to welcome an *haole* with a lei and a kiss," he explained.

Betty sat down.

"Meet Tillie," he said. Then to the Eurasian girl he added, "This is my new secretary. She'll be with me while Jane and her husband are back on the mainland."

Betty looked at the girl. She was beautiful. All the girls out here seemed to be beautiful. They made Betty feel like a waif just off the pickle boat. Tillie looked back at Betty and gave her a warm, friendly smile.

"Have you been here before?" The girl had a strange, but most pleasant accent.

"No. This is my first time."

"Do you like Hawaii?"

"Yes, but I don't think it likes me."

"No? Why not?" asked Tillie.

Betty glanced at Benning. She managed a helpless smile.

"She had an accident this afternoon," he said, then added, "Betty is a guest here at the hotel. She'll be staying for a few more days, I presume. Just look out for her."

"I'll do that," Tillie promised.

"No. I think you missed the point. I mean, for your own sake, look out for her. She's big trouble."

The Eurasian girl looked puzzled, first at Benning then at Betty.

"I just got through wrecking his car," Betty spoke up. She saw no reason for letting the matter go without explanation. And since confession was her mood at the moment, she added, "not only that, but I broke a fire hydrant and the city of Honolulu isn't very happy about that either. Mr. Benning is right. I'm big trouble."

"Mr. Benning is always right. It's only when we call him Jack that we make a human being out of him," Tillie declared.

"Okay," Benning laughed and glanced toward Betty. "From now on you call me Jack. Got it?"

"I'll try."

"Tillie is the gal in charge of things around the Surf Room," Jack said. "Anything you want, see Tillie. She's making some arrangements for us in connection with the reception. And, since you're a guest here, I might use you to see that things go right."

"That's a big order for me, considering how wrong I made things go this afternoon, Mr. — "

"Jack," he said quickly. "Remember I said to call me that."

"Yes, Jack," Betty said with some

difficulty. Then she knew right away, somehow, that the first effort was the hardest. She felt better the next time she called him Jack.

A scantily attired cocktail waitress came to the table. Betty ordered a small glass of white wine and Jack, who had been drinking a martini, ordered another one. Tillie excused herself and disappeared into the Surf Room to supervise preparations for dinner.

"This is one of my favorite places," said Jack.

"I can see why it would be," Betty replied as she looked at Diamond Head, its brown and green pastels tinted with yellow and red by the long rays of the setting sun. The beach was no longer crowded. A few hardy surfboarders were waiting and watching for one more large wave out by the reef. A spectacular sunset was developing. The temperature was perfect. All at once, for no logical reason that she could think of, Betty felt herself relaxing.

Stranger still was the fact that she and her boss were sitting here in silence, without seeming to feel the need for conversation — just enjoying each other's company. It gave her a warm glow inside. She glanced at him from the corner of her eyes and thought how handsome he was, gazing distantly out at the darkening blue ocean. She tried to guess what might be on his mind. At that moment the cocktail waitress brought their drinks.

"Cheers," said Jack, lifting his glass toward Betty. After a sip he spoke again. "With all that happened this afternoon we forgot the purpose of your errand. Did Cheryl say she was satisfied with the news release?"

"She hardly glanced at it," said Betty.

"Why not?" he asked.

"I really don't know. She gave it back to me without comment."

Betty did not say what she thought. She felt strongly that Cheryl Canton had been less interested in the release than in having Jack deliver it to her in person. When Betty showed up in his place, the girl was visibly provoked.

"Cheryl can be temperamental at times," he remarked.

"I know," said Betty and instantly wished she hadn't. Whatever was between

Jack and the Canton girl was none of her business. Jack glanced at her, a faint smile on his lips. Then he said:

"If she had wanted any changes in the release I suppose she would have said so. Okay, send it to the papers in the morning."

"Yes, sir."

"And don't call me, sir! The name is Jack, to you and the others in the office. Get it?"

"Yes . . . Jack," she said.

She enjoyed the wine as they sat there watching the lowering sun paint final touches on the sky. Then suddenly the great orange and red disc disappeared into the ocean and darkness came over the area. The torch lights along the sea wall were lit and the lights began to twinkle all along the crescent of Waikiki. She still wondered what her boss wanted with her, but she decided he would let her know in due time. Instead, he ordered another drink for both of them. When Tillie happened by a few minutes later, he spoke to her.

"What's for dinner?"

"It's steak night."

46

"Good. I feel like a steak," He looked at Betty questioningly. "What would you like?"

She was so surprised at being invited to have dinner with him that she did not know what to say for a moment. Then she echoed, "I guess a steak."

"After what you've been through, I think you need one. Keep a table for us, Tillie, will you please?"

"It's already reserved and waiting," the hostess smiled.

Betty figured she would have to wait a bit longer to find out why he was staying here with her. He certainly gave her no inkling while they finished their drinks and moved into a table for two by the dance floor in the Surf Room. The restaurant was filling up rapidly, mostly with extremely well-dressed older people.

"Do many tourists come to this hotel?" she asked, looking around.

"Yes, but most of these you see in here for dinner are spending the winter."

"They must be rich."

"Many are. Many have been coming here for years. See that couple over there.

47

The tanned, white-haired gentleman. That's Mr. and Mrs. Blackman. He ships his car out every winter because he doesn't want to bother renting one here. The Kensingtons, sitting opposite us across the dance floor, are English. They have a villa on the Riviera, but come here for the winter. You may have recognized the tall thin fellow seated near the entrance. That's Frank Esswein, the composer. He's written a number of scores for motion pictures, among other things."

"Where is he?" Betty looked around impressed. "I have some of his music. He's quite good."

She was amazed at the number of people Jack Benning knew. Not only that, but how many knew him. A half dozen people had waved or nodded greetings to him while they had been seated outside before dinner. Three had said 'hello' to him as they passed by the dinner table and he in turn had called them by their first names.

While they ate their dinners, Jack told her about the other hotels along the beach. They were, with one exception, owned by Japanese interests, but were operated under contract by Americans. He handled some public relations duties for Kokusai Denki in this area. He filled her in on how much the tourist industry had expanded in recent years and, in doing so, made it sound most interesting. Jack Benning was a smart man. She began to understand why he was making a success of his public relations agency here in the Islands.

At seven o'clock the Kahauanui Lake Trio came on and began playing and singing songs of the islands. The music was soft and restful, not the raucous sounds popular in many other places. Betty pronounced the musicians quite good.

"A while ago you said you know about Esswein. Do you know music?" Jack asked, looking at her.

"A little. My father was a music teacher so I guess I come by it naturally."

"Do you play an instrument?"

"Yes. The piano," she told him.

"What else is there about you that I should know?" he asked.

"Nothing I can think of." Then as

an afterthought she added, "Do you remember that Japanese language course you sent to Mr. Placer, the one with the cassettes?"

"Yes. How did old George do with it?" Jack laughed.

"He didn't do anything, so I asked if I could borrow it. I took it home and studied it several times a week." The real reason she had done so was to fill the lonely evenings after she and Lon Holderness had split up. It helped get her mind off of her heartbreak and disappointment.

"Good for you!" Jack seemed delighted. "We meet a lot of Japanese in our work. Do you speak it well?"

"*Watakushi nihon go wa sukoshi hanashimasu. Wakarimasu ka.*" 'I speak a little Japanese. Do you understand? she said.

"*Hi,*" 'yes' Jack replied.

They looked at each other and smiled. A small surge of excitement raced through her. Again, they seemed to communicate with each other, as they had while sitting on the lanai looking at the sunset — a communication that did not need words.

An unspoken awareness of each other. An enjoyment of each other's company.

"Hey, they're playing your song," he said suddenly.

The spell was broken. Betty wondered if she had been deluding herself into thinking that Jack had felt the same sensation as had she. She resolved to use her head more than her instinct when it came to assessing her boss. But what happened next threw her into even more confusion.

"Shall we dance?" he asked.

He did not wait for an answer. Before she knew it they were on the dance floor, his arm gently, but firmly around her waist. Betty felt his strength as he held her to him. She rested her left arm across his broad shoulders. Suddenly she felt a strong physical attraction to this man. His muscular body and the easy rhythm of his movement conveyed the feeling of strength and grace. She was drawn to him against her will. They danced well together. She followed his lead perfectly. Several admiring glances came their way from those at the dining tables. Then she remembered to ask him a question.

"What do you mean, my song?"

"They're playing the Princess Pupule."

"Who and what is the Princess Pupule? You used that term before with me." She liked the song's lilting melody and good beat.

"It means the Princess ding-a-ling, nutsy, or whatever you wish. Pupule is the Hawaiian word for crazy."

"Well! Thanks a bundle!" She drew back and looked up at him, her eyes narrow with reproach.

"The Princess was also a dish," he smiled.

Betty found herself disarmed, before she could even start being angry. His dark eyes twinkled as he gazed down at her. His arm tightened ever so slightly around her waist. Betty's attitude toward her new boss was thrown into further confusion. She did not know what to think of him. She could not understand why he was spending the evening with her when, less than three hours ago, she had wrecked his car and caused him no end of trouble. On top of that he had called her cuckoo. Yet, now he was warm and intimate and seemed to enjoy her company. What sort of a man was he anyway?

When the music ended he suggested they walk out to the sea wall. The Royal palms were swaying in the warm trade winds, as they were when Betty first arrived on the island of Oahu, and she felt that magic and romance might be just beyond. The night sky was filled with winking constellations. Soft Hawaiian music mingled with the sounds of the surf breaking on the sand. Betty looked at it all and was overcome by its beauty.

"I never believed Hawaii could be so lovely," she exclaimed.

"It's the only place in the world I know of that lives up to its advance billing. These Islands start selling themselves the minute a person lands here. Or did you notice that when you arrived?" he glanced at her.

"So many things have happened in the short time I've been here that I haven't really thought about it," she said woefully.

"Maybe tomorrow will be a better day." He glanced at his wrist watch.

"I'd better let you turn in." Then he added in a bantering tone, "So you won't be late again in the morning."

"Please," she begged with a smile, "I'm trying hard to be good."

They walked through the lobby to the elevator. And then, again to Betty's further amazement, he gave her a goodnight kiss.

"Aloha," he said. "Until we meet again."

The elevator door closed. Betty rode to the third floor in a daze, the warm touch of his lips still vibrating on hers. Of all the incredible things that had happened to her today, his kissing her had to be the climax. Why had he done it? Was it as he had said just an old Hawaiian custom with little or no meaning? Or what? She had learned quite a lot about her new boss. But what she had learned she did not understand.

As she went down the hall to her room, she began to feel a great weariness, both mentally and physically. Enough had happened to her, in one day, to make it seem weeks, even months ago that she had left her room this morning to report to her new job. She fumbled with the key. Then she heard the phone inside ringing. She realized that it had been ringing before she became consciously aware of it. She tried desperately to get the door open. When, finally, she succeeded and rushed to the phone there was no one at the other end.

"Now what?" she said to herself as she stood there holding the receiver. She put it down and turned away. Then, from the corner of her eye, she saw a small amber light begin to glow on the telephone. Quickly she picked it up again and asked the operator what it was about.

"One moment, please. Mahalo," came the operator's voice. A moment later the operator came on again. "A Mr. Warson Graham wishes you to call him as soon as possible. His number is eight-seven-eight five-seven-three-five. You can dial that direct."

"Thank you." said Betty. For an instant she could not think who Warson Graham was, then she remembered the older man in the office. She dialed his number.

"Hello," Graham answered after a couple of rings.

"This is Betty Lane, Mr. Graham. You called me?" She was quite curious over what he might want with her at this hour.

"Oh yes. The newspaper has been trying to reach you. They couldn't locate Jack so they called me for help."

"What on earth does a newspaper want with me?" she asked in bewilderment.

"I don't quite understand it either. They said they had a picture of a girl identified as Betty Lane. It has something to do with an accident and a fire hydrant. They want a statement from you."

"I have no statement to make," she replied.

"You'd better tell them something — "

"But what? I had an accident. I hit a fire plug and it spouted water. And I remember now that a photographer took a picture of it and of me standing there. I was drenched."

"Really," said Graham, his interest aroused.

"There was nothing more to it than that," Betty told him.

"That's enough to make a good story and a good picture. Will you call them?"

"No."

"I think you should. We're in public relations, you know. We like to be honest and above board with the media. Jack would want you to."

"He knows all about it. I called him from the police station and he came right over. It was his car that I was driving."

"This gets better and better," Graham exclaimed.

"What do you mean by that?"

"You wrecked his car — ?"

"Yes. And I feel terrible about it."

"I think you had better call him right away and tell him the newspaper wants a statement from you. Maybe he can tell you what to say."

"But he just left five minutes ago. Besides, I don't know where he lives."

"Let me get this straight," said Graham after a shocked silence. "Jack was with you at the hotel, just now?"

"Yes."

"Look, Betty. Just leave me out of this. I didn't hear a thing. Understand? But in the interest of good press relations I must call the right editor back. I'll tell

57

him he can reach you now. The rest is up to you."

"Never mind. I'll make the call," she said and hung up.

Betty knew about public relations. It was not diplomatic to ignore an inquiry from the media. She pondered, for a moment, as to what she might give in the way of a statement. The truth. It was the only thing she knew to do. She looked up the number of the newspaper office and dialed. A moment later, Betty was connected with the newspaper office. She identified herself.

"Yes, Miss Lane," came a man's voice. "We have a story that we got from the police blotter and a picture that one of our photographers just happened by in time to get. It shows you and the wrecked car. And it shows the fire hydrant making quite a fountain."

"I know about it," she assured him bitterly.

"We want to know one thing. How did you happend to be driving the wrong way on the one-way street?"

"I didn't know it was one way."

"Was it plainly marked?"

"I don't know that either."

"If it had been you would have seen the sign. Wouldn't you?"

"I guess so," she admitted.

"That's what we wanted to know. Maybe we can get a picture showing poor markings and perhaps the City Hall will do something about it to prevent others from making the same mistake."

"Are you going to use the picture?" she asked.

"The one of you standing in the shower by the side of the curb is a beauty, Miss Lane. Yes, we're going to use it. It will be on the front page in tomorrow morning's paper. Thank you and good night."

The receiver went dead in Betty's hand. She dropped it and sank to the bed. She groaned as she sat there, slowly wagging her head from side to side. Was all of this really happening to her? Maybe she'd wake up in the morning and learn that she had had a bad nightmare!

4

BETTY arrived early and out of breath at the office next morning. It was a quarter of nine. No one was there and she had no key. So she cooled her heels in the hallway for nearly fifteen minutes, until Billy Everett arrived and unlocked the door. The first thing he did, when they were inside, was to produce a morning paper and point at the picture on page one.

"What happened? Am I mistaken, or is that really Jack's Thunderbird? I couldn't believe what I saw."

Betty looked at the picture. It showed her standing soaked beside the Thunderbird, the fire hydrant still spouting a fountain. The caption was fairly factual but, in quoting Betty, it made her seem to be faulting the Street and Highway Department for not marking the one way street more clearly.

"I didn't blame it on anybody but myself," she said indignantly. "They

60

got that part wrong."

At that moment Audrey Ching came in. She had seen the paper at home and couldn't wait to hear about it from Betty. Audrey and Billy were plying her with questions when Warson Graham came in.

"Good morning," he said to all of them, then he glanced at Betty with a significant smile and sat down at his desk without joining the other two at Betty's desk.

"Hey, didn't you see this about Betty?" Billy called over to Warson.

"Yes. I know about it. I was in touch with her last night," said Warson and turned to some correspondence on his desk.

"How did you happen to be driving Jack's car?" asked Audrey.

"He sent me to take a release to a girl by the name of Cheryl Canton and get her approval of it."

"Cheryl — ?" said Audrey, surprised.

"Yes. Do you know her?"

"Everyone around here knows Cheryl Canton. You had better believe it! Her family owns one of our largest accounts.

I'm surprised that Jack didn't take it out to her in person."

"He was busy with something. That's why he asked me to go."

"What did Cheryl say when you came in?" Audrey was quite curious about that.

"She asked the same thing you did. Why Jack hadn't brought it himself."

"I'll bet she did!" Audrey and Billy exchanged glances.

At that moment Jack entered. His presence had the same effect as a strong atmospheric disturbance. Billy hurried to his desk and sat down. Audrey grinned at Jack, said "good morning" then went to her desk. Jack glared at Betty.

"Will you come into my office please?" His tone was foreboding.

Betty followed him in. At his command she closed the door. He ordered her to sit down. He sat behind his desk, studying her for a long moment. There was controlled fury in his voice when he finally spoke to her.

"Nobody — but nobody!" he said, "has caused me so much trouble in a twenty-four hour period as you have."

"I — I'm sorry, Mr. Benning — "

"I told you to call me Jack!" he shouted.

"Yes, Jack!" she whispered.

He grabbed up the morning paper from his desk and jabbed a finger at the picture on page one. "Why, in the name of heaven, did you put the shaft to City Hall? Those fellows are our friends. And now you come along and give them the business for not marking a one way street. What in hell were you trying to do? Weasel out of the thing?"

"Oh no." She pleaded with agony in her eyes. "I admitted it was my fault. I told you that last night."

"Then why did you say what you did to the paper?"

"I — I didn't put it that way. The man I talked with put words in my mouth," she said lamely.

"Why did you call the paper in the first place?" he demanded.

"I didn't. Right after you left I got a call in my room. It was from Mr. Graham. He said the paper had been trying to reach me but couldn't. So they called him. He asked if I would call them back right away, in the interest of good press relations. And that's the truth, Mr. Ben — Jack. Ask Mr. Graham. I didn't want to talk to anybody after you left me at the elevator." She looked down unhappily, not wanting to face her boss's angry eyes.

"Hummmm," said Jack, after thinking it over. "What you say has the ring of truth. Okay, maybe I can smooth some ruffled feathers at City Hall. After all, the call I made got you released from the gendarmes yesterday. They didn't expect to get slammed for their help."

"I'm sorry." It seemed to Betty that she had been saying that almost ever since reporting to work at Benning & Associates yesterday morning.

"Let's get on with the day's work. We have a lot to do toward getting ready for the reception Thursday evening. That will be all for now. I'll have some letters to dictate later this morning or afternoon."

Betty understood that she was being sent back to her desk. And she was grateful to be dismissed. She needed some time to collect her wits. Even with such an inauspicious beginning, the morning turned out better than she had hoped. She had time to scan the want ads in the paper, looking for an apartment to share with some other girl. She was going broke by staying at the hotel and there remained a fire hydrant to pay for, even if she got out of having to pay a fine for traffic violations.

"What are you looking for?" Audrey asked, coming by Betty's desk later in the morning and observing her interest in the want-ad section.

"I have to move. And fast. I can't afford the hotel room rate."

"What are you looking for?"

"I'd like to get an apartment that I can share with another girl or two."

Audrey said nothing for a moment, then, "Let me think something over."

Without adding any comment to the remark she went back to her desk. Betty continued to search the want ad section, but with no results. She would try again tomorrow. But just before noon Audrey called to her.

"I'm free for dinner tonight, Betty. Would you like to join me? I have

65

something that might interest you."

"Sure. Thanks, Audrey. I'm free. I'm always free." She had no idea what the Chinese girl might have in mind.

"You don't know your way around out here yet, so why don't I pick you up at about seven o'clock. I have a car. Meet me at the drive-in entrance to the hotel. Does that suit?"

"Yes. I'll be there," said Betty.

That arrangement, however, had to be altered after lunch. Jack called her into his office, dictated some letters, then told her he wanted her to talk with Tillie in the Surf Room this evening about some further arrangements for the reception.

"Have dinner there and put it on my charge account," he added.

"Yes, sir. I mean, Jack. Audrey and I were to have dinner together, but — "

Audrey? Fine. You two go ahead and have dinner. Sign the check for both of you. Audrey knows Tillie and she can be of help. Here's a list of pupus and other things I want you to check off with Tillie." He handed her a list.

"What's a pupu?" asked Betty, glancing at the list that contained hors d'hoeuvres, flower arrangements and a list of mixed drinks to be available at the bar.

"Pupus are hors d'hoeuvres."

"Hawaiian hors d'hoeuvres," Betty commented, smiling.

"Right," and with that Jack left the office with the information that he would not be back that afternoon. He would be, he said, out at the Canton's for the later afternoon and evening, just in case he needed to be reached.

Betty felt a sudden shock at the mention of the Canton name. Good heavens! With everything that had been going on she had forgotten completely about the release. It should have been sent in last night. After Jack had gone, Betty got Audrey aside and confided in her.

"Where is the release?" Audrey asked.

"It's somewhere around here." Betty began digging frantically among papers on her desk.

"Is it long?"

"No. A couple of paragraphs."

"Let me have it. I'll phone it in. I have a friend in the society section."

Betty found it and gave it to Audrey who made a telephone call. It was a bit late getting in but, with Audrey's connection, it was assured of making the paper in the morning. Betty drew a sigh of relief.

"I must be going nuts," she told Audrey.

"Why so?"

"I would never forget an assignment like that, sending a simple news release. I did it many times in my job back in St. Louis. What worries me all of a sudden is my own disorganized state. I never used to be this way."

"It's just that you've been getting squared away out here in Hawaii," Audrey suggested.

"Whatever it is, I've got to get hold of myself. Simply got to!" Betty declared.

This was not like her and she knew it. She hated being so upset that she could forget her job. She resolved to calm down, to get control of herself and to get control of the events that seemed to have taken over her life. Damned if she was going to give in to adversity. To Audrey, she added:

"Jack said for the two of us to have dinner in the Surf Room. He's buying.

We're to talk to that girl whose name is Tillie about some arrangements for a cocktail party."

"That's the best offer I've had all day. I like that restaurant and I like Tillie. Okay, gal, see you there around six thirty."

That evening Betty and Audrey had dinner in the Surf Room. They went over arrangements for the party with Tillie, as Jack had asked them to do. Tillie assured them that everything would be attended to including the placement of a small spinet piano in the room.

"He didn't say anything about that," Betty spoke up.

"No. He called me before you two came in for dinner and said he had forgotten to mention it to you."

"He's never had a piano at one of these affairs before," Audrey commented. "Who's going to play it?"

Tillie shook her head. She didn't know. Betty didn't know either but all at once a tiny suspicion leaped into her mind. She remembered telling Jack that she played. Could he be expecting her to entertain? She was not accustomed to that sort of thing. In addition she was out of practice. Jack took an awful lot for granted. She hoped she was wrong, that it was just her imagination — the last thing she had ever thought of doing was playing the piano to entertain public relations clients.

"I'll just bet I'm the patsy," Betty remarked, more as if she were thinking out loud.

"What's that supposed to mean?" asked the Chinese girl.

"I happened to remark to Jack that I play. Do you think — "

"Why of course! That explains it. Jack believes in using everyone's talent around the office. One time he even had me do a dance during a presentation to a prospective new client. He dressed me up in a mandarin jacket and had me hold up posters. It was the craziest idea I ever heard of," said Audrey.

"Did you get the account?" Betty smiled.

"Yes. The Land and Development client. So you can't quarrel with success. Jack knows what he's doing, at least for the past four years."

"What was he doing before that?" asked Betty.

"I don't know. He came out here from California and started to work for Mr. Sullivan who had the public relations agency at that time. Jack bought it from him and changed the name to Benning. He makes friends easily and he knows his business. But around the office he can be a tyrant at times. He believes in efficiency. He's one of the most organized men I've known and he can't understand why everyone isn't that way."

"How old is he? Do you know?" asked Betty.

"I think he's twenty-seven or twenty-eight."

"He's done very well for that age."

"He had some money when he arrived, so I'm told. That's how he happened to buy out Mr. Sullivan. I think he inherited something from his father. I have never heard the full story," said Audrey.

After Tillie left and the girls had finished their dinners Audrey told Betty why she had wanted to visit with her.

"My sister is getting married next

71

Monday. She and I have been living together and, of course, she'll be moving out. I had thought eventually of asking someone to move in with me, share the apartment, but I've been in no hurry. However, you say you're looking for a place?" Audrey stopped and eyed Betty.

"Yes."

"Well then, I have a one bedroom apartment on the Ala Wai just ocean side of Kalakaua. It's within walking distance of the office and the shopping center. Would you be interested?"

"I think so," she said tentatively. "Would you want me as a roommate?"

Audrey smiled. "Why not? Is there any reason why we couldn't get along?"

"I don't know of any."

"You'll want to see the apartment before making up your mind," said Audrey. "If you wish, we can drive over there now. It's a mess because my sister's clothes are strewn all over the place. You know what getting ready for a wedding can mean."

Betty thought she knew. She had planned it all many times in her mind during the months she thought she and

Lon were engaged and would soon announce their plans for the wedding. For a brief moment she was swept back to those bittersweet days followed by agony and despair. Betty forced herself to quit thinking about it.

After dinner they drove in Audrey's car to the apartment. It was on the eleventh floor of a twenty-two story building. The moment they walked in, Betty knew she would like to live here.

Beyond a large sliding glass door that led out onto a small lanai was a view of the lights of Honolulu spread out and dazzling below. The living room and dining-L were comfortably and casually furnished in white rattan furniture, a red and black Oriental cabinet and a profusion of green planters; and always there was the magnificent view from any place in the room. The bedroom was small but adequate, taken up mainly by a queen size bed. Two closets and a dressing table and a chest of drawers filled up the room. One straight chair stood on one side of the bed and on the other side was a table and night lamp.

"It's beautiful," said Betty.

"There's a small swimming pool at the side of the building. And laundry facilities in the basement. There is twenty-four hour security. You noticed when we came in that the doorman had to unlock the main entrance," Audrey smiled. "You don't have to say right now if you want to move in with me. Think it over. Let me know in a day or two."

"I'm sure I'd like it here," said Betty without hesitation.

"Go out there on the lanai and sit down. I'll whip us up an after dinner drink of some sort."

Betty went to the lanai and sat in a comfortable canvas chair. She could not keep her eyes off of the myriad of lights that seemed to mingle with the stars in the dark blue Hawaiian sky. Below and on the other side of the street was a broad canal-looking body of water beyond a sea wall. On the opposite side were more buildings and apartments.

"Try this," said Audrey coming out and handing Betty a tall cold glass filled with polynesian flavors and a light rum.

"It's delicious. What is it?" asked Betty, after a sip.

"That's what they call Menehune juice."

"What is Menehune juice?" Betty laughed.

"Menehune is an Hawaiian elf. Little imaginary people like the Leprechans of Ireland."

"Now I know two things. A Menehune and a Princess Pupule," Betty commented.

"Where did you find out about the Princess?"

"That's what our boss called me last night," Betty explained.

"Jack? Last night? What did he call you that for?" Audrey's curiosity was suddenly aroused.

"For getting into such a scrape with his car and for all the other trouble I caused him, I guess. Anyway, they played that song and he insisted on dancing."

"Hey, back up! What's all this? You and Jack went dancing?" Audrey looked at her with wonder.

"After we left the police station and his wrecked car he took me to the hotel. Then he decided to stay and have dinner, so we ate where you and I did this evening. That's where he introduced me to Tillie."

"Oh boy! Wait till this gets out!" Audrey exclaimed with obvious glee.

"Is it something wrong I did?" Betty was perplexed.

"I guess you could call it that. But there was nothing wrong about it. Quite the contrary. It's a lesson on how to get a dinner date with Jack Benning. Just go out and wreck his car." Audrey laughed hard for a moment, then she looked at Betty. "You know, I think I'm going to enjoy having you as my roommate."

They visited a while longer then Audrey drove Betty back to the hotel. It was still only nine o'clock and Betty was not sleepy. She wanted another look at that great view of Waikiki that she had seen with Jack last night. She walked through the lobby and out along the ocean lawn to the Mai Tai bar area. The salt air was cool but comfortable. She stood at the sea wall and looked at the great dark bulk of Diamond Head brooding under the topical stars. There was a wonder and beauty in the night. What a lovely spot indeed, just as Jack had said.

76

While she was standing there a Japanese couple came to the sea wall and stared out at the scene. They spoke Japanese and Betty immediately started listening in, not to eavesdrop but to practice her Japanese language study. The wife, as nearly as Betty could understand, had asked her husband where Diamond Head was.

"*Soko, omou,*" 'there, I think,' he said, pointing.

"*Hi, so desu,*" 'yes, that is so,' Betty spoke up helpfully.

The couple looked at her, pleasantly surprised.

"*Nihon hanashimasu ka.*" 'do you speak Japanese?' the man asked.

"*Sukoshi,*" 'a little,' Betty replied.

The three of them stood there a while longer talking. Betty was not able to follow much of the conversation but she did well enough to have them compliment her. Then the man addressed her in English.

"You do very well in our language," he said politely. "Where did you learn?"

"I've been studying for several months."

"Have you ever been to Japan?"

"No. But I hope to go sometime."

"If you do, we hope to see you there. I come to Hawaii on business, occasionally. Do you live here?" he asked.

"I do now," Betty explained. "But I've just moved here from St. Louis. I work for a public relation agency."

"Oh? What one?"

"Benning & Associates."

"What a coincidence. I am with Kokusai Denki and I'm here on business with Jack. We're having a reception day after tomorrow here at the hotel."

"Yes, I know about it. My name is Betty Lane and I'll be at the reception."

"It's a pleasure meeting you. I'm Edward Kobayashi and this is my wife, Hisako."

Betty and the Japanese lady smiled at each other.

"May we offer you an after-dinner drink?" asked Kobayashi.

Betty accepted the invitation mainly because it was an opportunity to continue her Japanese practice, though it was quickly apparent that Kobayashi was much more proficient in English than she was in Japanese. Nevertheless, as they sat at a table by the bar Betty enjoyed talking with them in their language. Mrs. Kobayashi spoke no English at all.

"My wife and I just arrived an hour ago from Tokyo. Jack knows we're coming. I half expected him to show up at the hotel this evening," Kobayashi remarked. "But meeting you is welcome enough from Benning & Associates."

"*Arigato gozeimus*," 'thank you.' Betty replied.

Kobayashi had hardly gotten the words out of his mouth when Jack did show up. And with him was Cheryl Canton. Jack looked at Betty, then at the Kobayashis questioningly.

"I see you've met my secretary," he remarked.

"Yes, and she's delightful." Quickly Kobayashi turned to Cheryl and bowed graciously. "Miss Canton, how good to see you again."

Betty was amazed that they all knew each other. She had no inkling how the Canton girl fitted in, but it was obvious that she was no stranger to the Kobayashis. Betty had the feeling that she would find out a lot more about Miss Canton and that she probably fitted in

79

a lot more than she might think.

Jack and Cheryl joined them at the table and ordered drinks. For a few moments most of the conversation was between Jack and Kobayashi about the upcoming reception. The Japanese man wanted Jack to organize a trade mission of men from Hawaii and the Mainland. They would visit Japan with two objectives in mind. One would be to visit with Japanese business men who might be interested in American investments both in Hawaii and on the Mainland. The other would be to help the Americans establish greater markets in Japan. After a bit, Kobayashi suggested they continue their business discussion in the morning in Jack's office.

"So here's to seeing you all again. We always enjoy coming to Hawaii," Kobayashi raised his glass.

They all drank to the toast.

"I'm curious as to how you happened to meet my secretary," said Jack.

"Pure coincidence. We were standing right over there discussing Diamond Head. My wife asked me a question as to its location. I don't see too well at night and Miss Lane, who was standing nearby, was kind enough to confirm what I told the Okusan. She spoke to us in Japanese."

"Very good of her to look after you," said Jack, casting a complimentary glance toward Betty.

"Miss Lane seems to be helpful, indeed, for only working for you for two days. I saw the publicity she attracted for the agency in the paper this morning," said Cheryl.

"That was unfortunate and I'm sorry about it," Betty said instantly.

"Was it really! It was one way of calling attention to yourself." There was contempt in Cheryl's voice.

Betty glanced at the girl quickly. Cheryl's smoldering eyes met Betty's for only a split second but it was enough to make Betty wary of the girl. Quite obviously they rubbed each other the wrong way. Cheryl Canton was rich, beautiful and self-confident. Betty was none of those things.

She felt a sudden hot resentment of the brunette and just as quickly she tried to overcome it. Was it envy on her part,

81

she wondered. If so, she must get over it. She knew the heartache that could cause. She had the same feeling about Sylvia Shaw, the girl back in St. Louis whom Lon Holderness had suddenly married. Her best bet was to get out of there before the tense moment between her and Cheryl got worse.

"I'm afraid I should be turning in," said Betty. "I'm still not quite acclimated to Hawaii, especially after the cold weather I left behind in St. Louis." With that she stood up.

"Ah so," said Kobayashi. He arose and bowed.

"*Oyasmi nasai*," 'goodnight,' said Betty nodding first to Kobayashi and then to his wife.

"Goodnight, Betty," said Jack, then added blithely, "Remember we open at nine."

"Yes, sir — I'm sorry. I mean Jack."

Betty had spoken from reflex. She didn't intend her remark to emphasize any familiarity between her and her boss. But she saw by the lightening flash in Cheryl Canton's eyes that the girl had taken it as a deliberate offense. She added quickly and as conciliatorily as possible, "Goodnight, Miss Canton."

There was no reply from the girl. Betty hurried off. As she walked through the lobby she berated herself for not having behaved more diplomatically. She had enough problems without encouraging Cheryl's enmity.

And yet, despite her better judgment, the girl provoked a surge of anger in Betty. She was afraid it was based mainly on envy, as originally thought. And envy was one of the seven deadly sins.

Later, as she lay in bed, she prayed for help to get a clean heart and to have the right spirit renewed within her.

Betty's prayer for the right spirit was answered and prevailed in her until ten minutes after eleven the following morning.

5

BETTY entered the private office of her boss late the following morning. She had her pencil and stenographic pad in hand, ready to take dictation. She sat down in the chair beside his desk and waited while he glanced through some correspondence.

"You called . . . " she reminded him.

"Oh, yes." He looked up suddenly, saw her pencil and pad and said, "You won't need that. I want you to run an errand during your lunch hour."

"Please don't make me drive somewhere," she begged.

He laughed. " I won't. Cheryl Canton asked me to send you to Shirokiya. She wants a black medium-sized hoppi coat with white calligraphy."

Betty was startled by the assignment, but she quickly jotted down the instructions in shorthand. She sat beside Jack's desk studying it.

"Got it?" Jack glanced at her.

"Yes, but — "

"But what?"

"Where is Shirokiya and what is a hoppi coat?"

"Look. I haven't time to explain all of that. Ask Audrey or one of the fellows," he said impatiently. His mood had changed in a matter of seconds.

Betty left his office immediately, wondering as she had a dozen times in the past few days if she would ever learn to anticipate his moods. She sat down at her desk and pondered his order. The more she thought of it, the angrier it made her. The nerve of Cheryl Canton asking any man to send his secretary out to do personal shopping. And on her lunch hour, at that!

"I'm damned — !" Betty declared out loud.

"You're what?" Audrey called over to her.

Betty explained the situation. The Chinese girl listened then looked at Betty with amusement.

"All I can suggest is that you grin and bear it," said Audrey.

"Oh, I'll do it, all right," Betty fumed,

"but where is Shirokiya and what is a hoppi coat?"

Audrey explained that Shirokiya was a Japanese store on the second level of the Ala Moana shopping center, less than a three minute walk from the office. And all she had to do when she arrived there was ask to see their hoppi coats.

Betty set out at noon for Shirokiya. The instant she entered the store her eyes widened. It was the first truly Oriental mercantile establishment she had ever been in. She was fascinated with the color and profusion of articles for sale. The pungent odor of incense filled the air. She took a moment to look at the low, highly polished tables called *tsukue*, the *tatami* floor mats, *ikebana* flower arrangements and the jade and pearls in the jewelry cases. Then she asked a pretty almond-eyed Japanese sales girl where she might find hoppi coats.

"This way, please." The girl led her to another section of the store. "Here you are. Any particular size or color?"

"Yes. Medium size, black with white calligraphy," Betty told her, not sure what the calligraphy would turn out to be.

The girl looked through a rack of hoppi coats. Betty had seen designs of this sort before, back in St. Louis. They were short, shirt-like pictures of Japanese judo wrestlers, but until now she had never really known what they were.

"Here you are." The girl took one off the rack and held it up for Betty to see.

"*Kore kudasai*," 'Give me this one,' said Betty, taking the opportunity to practice her Japanese.

"Ah, you speak Japanese. How nice," said the girl pleasantly.

"*Sukoshi-no*," 'A little,' Betty replied.

"You have a good accent."

"Thank you."

"Is there anything else I can show you?"

"No. That will be all. But I would like to look around, if you don't mind. Incidentally what does that symbol on the coat stand for?"

"Friendship."

"That's a laugh," Betty commented drily, thinking of Cheryl.

"That will be fifteen dollah," said the girl.

All at once, Betty wondered how Cheryl wanted to pay for it. "I was asked to pick it up for someone. Maybe she has a charge account here. Her name is Cheryl Canton."

"I'll check it." The clerk went off. When she came back she reported that there was no charge account in that name. "But if you wish to open an account we will be happy — "

"No." Betty dug into her purse. She had eighteen dollars. To avoid further confusion or delay she handed the money to the girl.

"Thank you. I'll put it in a sack." With that the girl went off again. She was back, in a moment, with a receipt and a sack containing the hoppi coat.

Betty had one satisfaction as a result of her errand. She took time to walk along the mall, amazed at the conglomeration of shops and services. Oriental stores competed with occidental. There were clothes from Hong Kong and Fifth Avenue, furniture from the Philippines and Grand Rapids, Aloha fashions and

Paris imports. There was a Sears and a Woolworth's, a Ming's and a Musashiya, Palm Beach and Tahiti imports. And food from all over the world — grilled squid on a stick, hamburger on a bun, noodle shops and steakhouses, tea rooms and beer parlors, Wong's Okazu-Yo and Smitty's Pancake House. The Poi Bowl was only a few stops from a Dairy Queen.

But it was the throngs of people of every type and description that fascinated Betty the most. Large, happy-go-lucky Polynesian women with their small, brown children looking in store windows; well-dressed visitors from Australia and New Zealand; Japanese tourists with Japan Air Lines flight bags over their shoulders; Canadians, Americans, Chinese and Latin-Americans. Surely, she thought, Scheherezade in her Thousand and One Nights had never imagined such a colorful bazaar with such countless contrasts.

Betty was so intrigued by it all that she very nearly lost track of the time. Realizing that it was coming on one o'clock she grabbed a sandwich at a snack shop, had it put into a paper bag and hurried back to the office.

"Did you just come back from shopping for Miss Canton?" asked Billy Everett when she was back in the office.

"Yes. Jack sent me to buy a hoppi coat for her."

"Good. Let me have it. I have to take some material out to her and Jack said I should take this along."

"I paid fifteen dollars out of my own pocket for it. Will you tell her that?" asked Betty.

"Sure," said Billy and took off.

When Audrey returned from lunch she asked Betty how she had gotten along with her shopping.

"No problem, really, except that I had to pay for the hoppi coat myself. I guess Miss Canton will reimburse me."

"In time, no doubt."

"A funny thing," Betty mused. "Do you know what those Chinese or Japanese characters — I don't know which — meant?"

"There are several different things they put on hoppi coats."

"This one meant 'friendship.'"

Audrey laughed. "Maybe Cheryl is

90

going to give you that hoppi coat as a peace offering. Maybe she wants to make amends for being so high-handed with you."

"Do you really believe that?" asked Betty, wanting to believe it herself. She didn't want to be at odds with Cheryl Canton or anyone else.

"Cheryl is unpredictable. She just might surprise you. But I wouldn't count on it if I were you," Audrey advised.

Betty was not going to count on it, but at the same time she wanted to give Cheryl the benefit of the doubt. It would improve her own attitude. Her sudden anger over the assignment had not been good for her. It was another of the Seven Deadly Sins. She could not afford to carry thoughts such as that in her heart. They contained the seeds of self-destruction.

The remainder of the day and all of the next were devoted to getting ready for the reception. Jack had special assignments for everyone. Billy and Warson were to pay special attention to the men and Audrey and Betty were to see that the few wives who were coming were supplied with hors de'hoeuvres and drinks. Jack would be the major domo and would circulate among all the guests. The office closed at four o'clock and everyone was sent home to get ready to greet the guests.

Betty had the best of that arrangement, staying at the hotel and being within an elevator ride to the scene of the reception. Her one regret was that she did not have anything really suitable to wear. The only long dress, she had, looked rather plain along side the gorgeous gowns that she had seen during her short time on Oahu. But she made the best of it and was the first to arrive in the Queen Liliokalani suite on the second floor overlooking the ocean.

"Hello there," said Tillie when Betty came in.

The hostess was already there with Eiko, one of the Japanese waitresses from the Surf Room, who was beautifully dressed in a colorful Japanese kimono. Eiko would be serving drinks to the guests. Tillie was sensational as usual in a long, oriental type gown. Jose, the bartender, was already at work setting up bottles. And the buffet looked wonderfully tempting with all the shrimp, mushrooms and steam trays full of tiny sandwiches.

"Looks like you're all ready for us," Betty remarked.

"It's nothing. We take care of much larger crowds than this without any trouble at all," Tillie assured her.

Jack came in shortly and, within another five minutes, all the Benning Associates had reported in for duty. Jack inspected the arrangements and found them to be to his satisfaction. He smiled his approval to one and all.

"Okay, kids. Let's all do a good job. We're entertaining some very important people. It could mean a lot to all of us."

Betty had no idea who the very important people were, but she was determined to treat each and every one as if he were royalty. And that, she told herself firmly, included Cheryl Canton.

The guests began to arrive shortly after five. Like every group of people Betty had seen in Hawaii, it included

Americans and Asians, Islanders and Europeans.

Jack and the others introduced Betty to the guests as quickly as they could, but in such a gathering it was impossible for her to meet everyone. Being basically a social person, Betty did not hesitate to introduce herself, if someone smiled in her direction.

And a number of them did, especially one young man by the name of Nick Lyons who turned out to be head of the news department at one of the local television stations.

"You're the little gal who created quite a fountain over near the Freeway a few days ago," said Nick, a medium-sized young man with a good build, a handsome face and a small, well-trimmed mustache.

"Unfortunately, yes," Betty smiled helplessly.

"How come I haven't met you before?" asked Nick.

"I've only been working here since Monday." Betty told him. "I came from St. Louis to take Mrs. Kimura's place while she and her husband are gone."

"I know Jane. But Jack never mentioned that she had left."

"It's a temporary arrangement. She'll be back."

"When she comes back, how would you like to work for me?"

"You're kidding. Or maybe it's the cocktails," Betty laughed.

"Just try me."

At that moment Mr. and Mrs. Kobayashi came by and Betty spoke to them in Japanese.

"Hey! You speak Japanese! Maybe I'll hire you away from Jack before Jane returns," Nick Lyons exclaimed.

Betty introduced him to the Kobayashis and changed the subject. The four of them stood there visiting, with Betty interpreting as best she could for Mrs. Kobayashi. Her husband nodded his approval of Betty's efforts.

When Kobayashi learned that Nick was a news man on Oahu he took time to explain to him that he and Jack were trying to organize a trade mission to Japan. He thought it would be an advantageous venture for both countries at this time. He said he knew

Jack Benning would be excellent as the head of such a mission.

"And," Kobayashi added, "I might say I think Miss Lane, here, would be a welcome addition to such a party." And with that he gave Betty a gallant bow.

"If she goes, I'll go too," said Nick Lyons.

Betty laughed. The young fellow was obviously in his cups. But it was very flattering to her to have him show so much interest.

Cheryl and a distinguished looking man, possibly in his late thirties, showed up around six o'clock. Her escort turned out to be Clifford Yates, executive vice-president of the Iwalani Shipping Company that belonged to the Canton family. Betty smiled and nodded to Cheryl the first chance she got, but nothing came in return except a cold glance from the brunette.

About that time Jack got Betty aside.

"Do me a favor," he said.

"Sure."

"These parties can get a bit deadly toward the last. You said you could play the piano. How about some music?"

"Oh, really, Jack — " Betty had been afraid this might happen.

"Any kind of music will do."

"But I'm not in good practice and I've never entertained professionally," she protested.

"If you can play at all, I want you to," he said grimly, levelling his gaze at her.

Betty read the command in his dark eyes, with a feeling of resignation and hoping for the best, she went to the spinet and sat down. She prayed that she would not make a fool of herself and the Benning Agency. And with that she started to play the first thing that came to mind. It was Maple Leaf Rag, Scott Joplin's most famous composition. In no time at all Betty had the attention of nearly everyone in the room as she beat and thumped bass notes while her right hand carried the melodic tunes of ragtime music. She was not her father's daughter for nothing. Betty was good. Not great, but a good musician. The end of the tune brought a round of applause and cries for more.

"I was sure you could play but I didn't know you were this good," said Jack quietly. "Please keep on for awhile."

She played more of Joplin's music then switched to Cole Porter, Friml and Gershwin. A number of the guests gathered around the piano. And, looking up at one point, Betty saw Cheryl eyeing her narrowly. Eiko handed Betty a drink between numbers and, with Cheryl standing nearby, Betty made an attempt to be nice to the girl. She asked if Cheryl had anything especially in her mind that she would like Betty to play?

"You're doing quite well on your own," the girl snapped.

"That hoppi coat. Was it the right size and color?" Betty asked, determined to be sociable with the girl.

"Perfect. I gave it to our gardener for his birthday."

Betty nearly dropped her drink on the piano keyboard. This girl had sent her on an errand to buy a gift for her gardener? — ! Betty had to choke back her sudden fury. It was several moments before she was calm enough to resume playing. And when she did, it was with malevolence she did not know was in her.

"This little number is dedicated to you, Miss Canton," she said.

And with that she struck up an old time tune that had countless verses sung to it over, at least a century of American music. And as she played, Betty recited the doggerel that reminded her so aptly of Cheryl Canton.

"The busy bee pursues his soul,
With no regard for birth control,
And that is why at times like these,
There are so many little bees."

There was instant applause and laughter from an appreciative audience. All except Cheryl. No one noticed the glance of daggers between her and Betty. If the two girls had been dueling with hardware one or both would have been mutilated.

Betty stood up. The party was thinning out. She knew when to quit, even though a few persons urged her to continue. But Jack came to her rescue. He said she had done more than her share to entertain the guests. She deserved to relax with her drink.

Cheryl and her escort Clifford Yates

left a few minutes later. She was telling Jack a warm good night and bidding others adieu when Betty came into her line of sight. She froze and quickly glanced away.

No one saw Betty's response, which was to stick her tongue out at the girl. No one saw it, that is, except Jack.

"Was that necessary?" he demanded hotly when they were alone a few minutes later. The hotel help was cleaning up, Audrey and the two men from the office were relaxing over drinks. Jack had asked everyone to stay behind and to be his guest for dinner downstairs.

"Was what necessary?" asked Betty innocently.

"I saw you."

"Saw me what?"

"Saw you stick your tongue out at Cheryl."

"All I was doing was wetting my lips."

"Oh, yeah?" Jack was visibly shaken by Betty's attitude. For the first time in his life, he was at a loss for words. He had never had an employee who had proven so utterly disastrous, and yet was such a crack secretary. And now she had won the hearts of his clients with her friendly personality and her ability to entertain. Topping it all, she was alienating one of the part owners of his second largest account! Cheryl could get pretty vicious if she ever made up her mind to do so.

Jack resolved to let Betty know that he did not appreciate her misconduct, but for now he said nothing more about it.

"Come on, all of you. I told Tillie to save us a table downstairs. We can have something to eat, if anybody is still hungry, and have a post mortem over the reception. I want each of you to state your opinion as to how it went."

With that they adjourned to the Surf Room. The main topic, at first, was Betty's triumph at the piano. They all agreed she was great. All except Jack, who withheld his opinion. But he gave Betty a dark look and she knew the reason why.

This time, she knew for sure, she had overstepped her bounds. She felt terrible about it. Jack would have every right to fire her. When, she wondered, would she ever learn to control herself? She sat quietly while the others discussed the party.

The consensus was that the reception had gone over beautifully. Jack, himself, announced that he was pleased with it. He also said that he and Kobayashi had sounded out some of the guests about the possibility of a trade mission to Japan and had received favorable reaction.

"Good. Can I have the job of representing Benning & Associates on the trip?" Billy spoke up with a smile.

"Could be you'll have to go. We'll be making up the presentations. Someone has to be in charge of getting all the material out there in good time and good condition," said Jack.

Betty thought how nice it would be to go to Japan. But if anyone went it certainly wouldn't be her. Not after she was so rude to Cheryl Canton. She might be looking for another job instead.

By the end of the following day, which was Friday, Betty found herself exhausted. She had hoped to spend the weekend exploring Oahu, but all she looked forward to, at least at the moment, was getting out on the beach and into the warm sun.

At six o'clock when she was in her hotel room wondering where to go for dinner, she received a phone call.

"I wonder if I could be so lucky to find you at loose ends this evening? I'd like to take you to dinner," came a familiar voice, but one she could not place.

"Who is this?"

"Nick Lyons. We met last night at the cocktail party. Remember?"

"Sure, Nick. I remember."

"Can I pick you up? I know a cozy little French restaurant at Diamond Head. I think you'll enjoy it."

"That's kind of you, Nick." Betty hesitated only a moment. Why shouldn't she accept? "Yes. I'd like that very much."

"Good. Be in the hotel lobby at a quarter to eight. I'll see you there," he said and hung up.

Betty showered and dressed in a green printed two piece street-length silk. She had no idea about the restaurant but she did not want to wear the long dress she had on at the cocktail party last night.

At eight o'clock that evening Betty

found herself sitting with Nick Lyons in a small, but beautiful restaurant that looked out over the ocean and at the crescent of twinkling lights that was Waikiki. A French maitre d'hotel hovered beside them making sure that mademoiselle and monsieur were pleased with the location of the table. He made it sound as if the three of them were engaged in a conspiracy.

"It's beautiful," said Betty, as she looked around. "But then I'm beginning to think everything about Hawaii is beautiful." She remembered saying the same thing to Jack the other night and wondered if he and Cheryl were dining together now? Quickly she put that out of her mind.

"There are some raunchy spots, but generally you're right," said Nick.

Betty found him to be a pleasant young man and counted herself lucky to be invited to dinner with him. If it were not for him, she might never have gotten to see such a nice place as this. Nick ordered cocktails then turned to Betty.

"How did you happen to be Jack's secretary?"

Betty explained what happened then added, "And I had no idea it would work out when Mr. Placer, my boss in St. Louis, suggested it."

"I must say you made a smash hit with Jack Benning," Nick laughed.

For a second Betty was not sure what he meant. "I guess you mean my wrecking his car. It wasn't funny at the time and I'm still not out of it. I'll have to pay for the fire hydrant and probably a fine for driving wrong on a one-way street."

"Jack will help you get out of it. If he doesn't, I will."

"He already has helped to some extent, though why I'll never know. All I've done is cause him trouble."

"He can handle it. I've known him a long time. Knew him even back in Los Angeles."

"Is that where he's from?" asked Betty, interested.

"Yes. His father was a theatrical agent and a rather successful one. His mother was a singer and a dancer. But his father is gone now. Died in an auto accident seven or eight years ago. I don't know whatever became of his mother."

Betty felt a pang of sympathy for Jack, having lost her own father in the past year. Undoubtedly, it had affected him tremendously, just as her loss had affected her.

"I'm sure he must have felt a great loss," she remarked.

"Yes, he was beginning to work into his dad's business. But being a theatrical agent takes years of cultivating talent and, without his dad's personal connections and touch, Jack found it a tough row to hoe. Anyway, he's much better suited as a public relations man."

"He works hard, I know. And he expects the same from others."

"If he drives you too hard, come work for me," Nick grinned.

"After a crazy thing I did at the cocktail party last night he might even fire me," she said, remembering her clash with Cheryl.

"Not a chance. Jack won't let you go."

At that moment a waiter appeared with menus. Nick suggested several entrees, veal cordon bleu, sweetbreads, the Hawaiian Mahi Mahi or Opakapaka fish all of which, he assured her, were done very nicely here. While she was making up her mind Nick sent for two more cocktails.

"I'll bet there were plenty of fellows sorry to see you leave St. Louis," said Nick, after they had ordered. He eyed her appreciatively.

"No, not really." For an instant Betty was pensive, thinking back to Lon Holderness. A haunting nostalgia swept through her and for a second her heart throbbed with a familiar ache. No! She must not think of Lon. She wished Nick had not reminded her of her problem.

"Well, St. Louis's loss is Honolulu's gain. Aloha." He lifted the cocktail glass the waiter had set before him.

"Aloha," Betty lifted her glass back to him.

Nick proved to be full of interesting small talk and the dinner that was served was delicious. Nick ordered a bottle of Beaujolais to go with it. Betty was beginning to feel the effects of the drinks she'd already had. She sipped only part of one small glass of wine and refused an after-dinner drink.

"It's been a wonderful evening, Nick. Thank you so much for inviting me," she said when they arrived back at the hotel.

"My pleasure. I hope to see more of you soon," he smiled.

"Goodnight."

He threw a kiss as she entered the elevator. Smiling, she threw one back.

Late the following morning Betty lay face down in the light brown sand on Waikiki Beach in front of the hotel. She had slept soundly last night, but she was still tired from the great transition she had made during the past week. The sun felt good on her back and legs and caused her to doze from time to time.

During wakeful moments, she looked at the grains of sand just inches from her eyes. She disturbed them with her hand and watched them rearrange themselves. Her mind was resting along with her body. It was good to have this time by herself, even though she shared the beach with countless others whose voices came to her in many languages. How far away it all was from St. Louis. She dozed again.

And then, like a shot, she awoke. In the split second transition from sleep to wakefulness she thought she heard Lon's voice. She looked up quickly. Had she been dreaming or was this reality?

It could not be the latter. She must be suffering hallucinations. Nevertheless, she looked around, searching, hoping, knowing all along it was a cruel hoax brought on by her own imagination and longing. Yes, she admitted to herself at that moment, she still had that breathless feeling about Lon. She felt a wave of hopelessness. How was she ever going to break the chains that bound her to a lost love?

A moment later someone spoke her name. This time she was not dreaming. But neither was it Lon.

"I thought I might find you here," said Jack.

6

JACK wore a white beach coat, white swim trunks and sun glasses. His muscular, deeply tanned body drew admiring glances from both men and women who were walking nearby on the beach. Betty had known all along that he was good-looking, but it was not until now, seeing him in a swim suit, that she realized just how uncommonly handsome he was. He sat down beside her on the sand.

"I thought you might be interested to know that the insurance is going to take care of the fire hydrant as well as the car," he said. "I just found it out this morning."

"Golly! Thanks!" Betty sat up and brushed the sand off of her abdomen and legs.

"Don't thank me. Thank the insurance company."

"Thanks, Mr. Insurance Company, wherever you are," Betty laughed.

"Now if you can beat the rap on the careless driving charge, you'll have nothing to worry about." He smiled.

"You've made my day, just by telling me about the insurance. I'll worry about the other later." Betty was delighted and surprised with the information. She had fully expected to pay for the fire hydrant.

"What have you been doing? Have you gone any place? You could have taken today and tomorrow to see some of the island." Jack reclined on his side, supporting himself on one elbow.

"I was too tired. But I did see a most attractive French restaurant last night. Your friend Nick took me to it, out near Diamond head."

"Nick Lyons?" Jack looked at her peculiarly. "How did that happen?"

"He called me up and invited me."

After along pause, Jack said, "Be careful with Nick. He has a wife back in Los Angeles. They've been separated for a year and she won't give him a divorce."

"Oh?"

"How long have you been out in the

111

sun?" he changed the subject abruptly and began looking her over.

"About an hour. Why?"

"It's easy to get a burn your first time out."

"I'm using lotion."

"Then let me have it. You need some more."

Betty got out a bottle of sun tan lotion and handed it to him. He spread some on her shoulders and back and began rubbing it in. She felt a pleasantly warm sensation as his strong hands moved over her skin. It was more like a massage than an application of sunburn preventative. A new physical feeling toward Jack was stirring inside her — one she did not trust. There should be nothing but a friendly attitude and mutual respect between a man and his secretary. Just the same, she reveled under his ministration.

"There," he said when he finished. "I hope that helps. I've known people to end up in the hospital with too much sun."

Betty thanked him and put the lotion away, still exhilarated by the touch of his hand rubbing her skin with lotion.

"Care to walk up the beach with me? I'll show you where I live," said Jack.

"You live on Waikiki?" Betty was surprised without really knowing why. She had assumed that the beach was inhabited only by all the visitors.

"Yes. I have an apartment just three blocks from here on the other side of Kalakaua."

"I thought there were nothing but hotels along Waikiki."

"That's correct with one exception. The building I'm in has apartments and condominiums. It was built for that purpose just when things were beginning to develop out here. If you would like to see it, come along."

Betty pulled on a shirt that she was using for beachwear and returned the towel that had been given to her by one of the hotel beach boys. Then she hung her beach bag over her shoulder and she and Jack started out and up Waikiki. They went by the catamarans that take visitors out for an hour's ride, and by the great banyan tree in the court of the Moana where visitors sat at a bar and at tables eating and watching the

113

never-ending spectacle of the famous beach. Beyond the public facilities and the surfboard storage area in the Kuhio section of Waikiki, Jack directed her toward the sidewalk on the ocean side of Kalakaua Avenue. They went still farther, then he took her arm and led her across the street.

"Here we are. Foster Towers," he said.

"I had no idea you lived so close," Betty replied.

"It's convenient, and I like the beach atmosphere when I'm not working. It's nice to have a change from the world of business and commerce." He took her inside to the elevator.

Betty had not understood that he was going to show her his own apartment. She had thought he meant only the building in which he lived. And so, she was a bit nonplussed as they rode up to the eighth floor. His apartment was on the front of the building, looking out over the avenue and Waikiki beach. The view from the lanai was breathtaking, but it was the way he had furnished his apartment that gave her another insight as to what sort of man he might be.

This was not a south seas or oriental atmosphere at all. Except for the lanai which contained two lounges, a cocktail table and a captain's folding chair, the apartment inside was strictly American traditional. Along one wall was a large redwood bookcase above three compartments enclosed by doors. A large leather chair and ottoman, a comfortable looking overstuffed couch and a highly polished redwood desk dominated the living room. An oriental rug covered the floor. On another wall was a small mahogany service bar. It was strictly a man's domain even to the leathery odor in the air.

"It's beautiful," said Betty looking around. She noticed a picture of several young Navy officers in uniform and went over to examine it more closely. She turned to Jack. "You're the one in the center. Right? I didn't know you had been in the Navy."

"I took Naval Reserve Officers Training at college. They sent me and some others out here on a summer training cruise. I liked Hawaii immediately, though I had no idea of living here until later, when an opportunity in public relations came up."

Still looking at the picture, she remarked to herself how great he looked in the Navy uniform. It was enough to turn any girl's head. She was proud to have such a handsome man as her boss but she mistrusted the sudden flicker of something more inside her — a 'something' easily confused with a childish schoolgirlish crush. In someone older though, Betty admitted to herself, that 'something' could be compulsive, unadorned desire.

At that moment a buzzer sounded and Jack went to an intercom on the wall beside the door.

"Yes?"

He was silent a moment. Betty continued glancing around the room, intrigued at being able to look over her boss's private abode. Then she heard him speak again.

"Okay, Cheryl. Come on up."

Betty snapped to attention at the mention of the girl's name. She looked at Jack. He was visibly agitated. He glanced at her.

"Miss Canton is in the lobby. She's coming up."

"I'll go. I enjoyed seeing your apartment." Betty immediately headed for the door.

"Wait," said Jack. "I don't think it would be wise for the two of you to meet in the hallway or at the elevator."

"Is there a back way — ?"

"Don't be silly!" He shot her a look of disapproval. "Just wait here. She'll be up at any moment."

Any doubt that Betty might have had about Cheryl's attitude toward her was gone once and for all. Jack's concern told her plenty. He was much aware of the brunette's feeling toward Betty. And he suspected Betty of harboring similar thoughts toward Cheryl.

There was a knock at the door. Jack opened it. Cheryl breezed in, gave Jack a kiss and smiled up at him. Then she saw Betty. A storm gathered in her eyes.

"Well! You didn't tell me you had company!" She turned on Jack.

"Betty just came by to see the apartment. She needs to know more about apartment living because she's

117

moving out of the hotel shortly. She'll be living with Audrey Ching," he said.

The explanation did not quite ring true. Even Betty sensed that. He was making excuses for which there was no need. Unless — Betty hesitated even to entertain the thought — he had in these few days developed more than a casual interest in her, to the detriment of Miss Cheryl Canton. No. Betty simply could not believe that she was a rival of Cheryl's for Jack's affections.

"And besides, I was about to leave," Betty added. "It was nice seeing you again, Miss Canton." She went to the door.

"Have a good week-end, Betty," said Jack lamely.

It was the first time Betty had seen him ill at ease. She could not help smiling to herself as she went down on the elevator. Not because Jack was upset. But because Cheryl Canton was.

Looking back on the incident, Betty wondered just what it was that had involved her so much in a situation that was none of her business and in which she really had little interest. Oh, it was easy to understand how and why she had reacted to Cheryl the first time they had met at the girl's home. That and her other encounters with the brunette more than explained her attitude. But the puzzling thing was Jack's position between the two of them. She tried to put it out of her mind, but found herself comparing Jack to Lon Holderness.

But events contrived to help Betty in a more constructive way. The following Tuesday she checked out of the hotel and moved her belongings to Audrey's apartment. All that week she had learned new things about life in Hawaii: about her roommate and about the workings of Benning & Associates.

Audrey, though of Chinese ancestry, was thoroughly American. Except for two beautiful Chinese gowns, her wardrobe was suited, like those of other girls, to the salubrious climate and beach atmosphere. The two girls quickly discovered that they could easily exchange clothes, for they were about the same size. Audrey delighted in trying on Betty's dresses and insisted that Betty help herself to anything of hers that attracted her. Before

Betty knew it, their clothes became so integrated that she gave up trying to keep her dresses hung up on one side of the closet, as they had agreed at the outset. Audrey had little sense of organization in that respect. Betty concluded that it was because she was used to having her sister with her and that she considered her new roommate in the same light.

But there was one thing about Audrey that Betty had not realized. She was a born flirt who liked the boys and, judging from the number of dates she had, the boys liked her. She was light hearted, lots of fun, loved good food and always had cold beer in the refrigerator. She was sensuous and uninhibited around the apartment, frequently sleeping in her birthday suit, lounging in mini-panties and, even when neighbors from apartments along the hall dropped in to meet Betty, sitting with only a thin shirt covering her from her hips up. In the late afternoon, when they returned from the office, Audrey frequently took a bottle of beer out onto the lanai, propped her bare legs up on the railing and relaxed contentedly in the late afternoon sun.

"This," said Betty the first time she joined her roommate for a beer on the lanai, "is one of the very nice things about living here. Back home, there is no way that you can sit out and be comfortable."

"What about in the summer?" asked Audrey.

"Most of the time it's too hot."

"I can't imagine that."

It dawned on Betty that the girl really meant it. Audrey had lived her entire life in the Hawaiian islands. The only time she had been away was when she graduated from high school. Her parents had given her a week's trip along southern California along with eight other girl-graduates under a teacher chaperone. It had been a colossal bore, Audrey contended. The chaperone had taken them to Disneyland, a motion picture studio, one trip to the beach at Redondo where they almost froze in the cold water, and a one-day drive in a bus to see a large art exhibit in Laguna.

"I spent the whole time trying to figure out how I could get a date and get away from the chaperone," Audrey laughed.

"Did you succeed?" asked Betty.

"No. The closest I ever got to a boy was in a jam packed elevator."

While she was learning about her roommate, Betty was also learning that life on the island was a far cry from the habits and customs of home. She was delighted when turning the dial of her radio to come across a station that had as the identification to its news segment a perky little tune and a voice-over singing 'on the coconut wireless,' followed by a few bongs on what could have been an empty coconut. Television programs were at least a week behind those on the mainland. And the stations paid little attention to schedules. More than once Betty turned on a program only to discover that it had started ten or fifteen minutes earlier, or that it would be coming up later. She listened with interest to stations that carried nothing but Japanese programs and one radio station specialized in nothing but Hawaiian music.

Back in St. Louis, she could not remember when she had heard or read anything of interest about the state legislature. In Hawaii, the activity in the State and Municipal government was news of equal importance to the passage of vital legislation in the Nation's Capitol. Each addition of the newspapers carried complete records of the weather and temperatures in the major cities back on the mainland under the headline, 'aren't you glad you're in Hawaii?'

Yes, Betty was glad, she agreed, except for the rueful yearning that still plagued her for happiness in St. Louis. That, she recognized, was less a matter of geography than it was of human relationships.

Audrey took her shopping for groceries and taught her to look for the bargains. Bargains were something Betty quickly learned were desperately needed. She could not believe some of the prices. And as for the premium cuts of steak and certain sea food, forget it! It was the sea food that Betty could not understand. Mahi-mahi, opakapaka, humuhumunukunukuapuaa — names she could not even pronounce — were all Hawaiian fish but they, too were expensive. Salmon and Alaskan King Crab were what you bought when you suddenly came into money.

But the girls were far from starving. Betty had never seen a refrigerator that was so well provisioned. Audrey, possibly because of an atavistic shrewdness inherited from generations of Chinese, was sensible about what they bought and what she recommended to Betty. On top of that, Audrey was invited out to dinner several times a week. She assured Betty that she would be too, once she got acquainted.

"I don't know about that," said Betty, late one night when Audrey had returned from a date. Betty had sat up, reading a book.

"Why not? You've got blonde hair and that goes big out here, especially with Orientals and Polynesians. You've got most attractive features and a shape that lots of girls would give their birthright to own. So, why not? Answer me that," the Chinese girl demanded.

Betty was in a relaxed mood and all at once without intending to, she found herself confiding in her roommate — something she had done with only one other person: Peg Waters, her good friend back in St. Louis.

"I was in love with a young man back in St. Louis. Still am, I'm afraid. But it didn't work out. He married another girl." The instant she had spoken those words she was sorry. She did not want to burden others with her problem, nor did she want others even to know about it. It was a matter of pride, she guessed.

Audrey stared at her for a long moment.

"So that's what's been bothering you!" she exclaimed. "Why didn't I think of it?"

"Why should you?" asked Betty, startled by the girl's attitude.

"We've been wondering about you at the office and I've been wondering even more since you moved in with me. There's been something about you. Some reticence. Something none of us could put our fingers on. So, you've been carrying the torch! Of course. That explains everything." She grinned.

"What do you mean by that?" Betty was a bit put out with Audrey.

"Just what I said. I've been wondering what you were holding back. And now I know." Suddenly her voice became

125

gentle. "Look, sweetie, no man is worth worrying over that much."

"I was in love with him."

"You still are. It shows all over, now that I know the reason."

Betty looked away. Audrey moved over and embraced her.

"Look, whoever that guy was, he was never your true love. Have you ever thought of it that way? If he had been, you'd be married to him."

Tears filled Betty's eyes. But it was a relief, somehow to have gotten it out. She never could have found a more understanding person than this Chinese girl who suddenly gave her comfort with her arms.

"Oh, Audrey, I've been so unhappy," Betty sobbed.

"Don't worry. We're going to do something about that, starting right away."

Audrey was as good as her word. The following week-end she took Betty with her to the windward side of the island to attend a *hukilau*, a native fishing party which turned into an all night orgy of eating, drinking and hula dancing. It was held on a beach in a beautiful bay and Betty, wearing a lavender vanda orchid lei that had been given to her upon their arrival, was taken by the extreme friendliness of everyone Audrey introduced her to. She was able to abandon her troubles and enjoy the festivities.

"So you're Jack's new secretary," said Katherine Knox, an older girl whom Betty had met earlier in the evening.

Betty nodded and smiled.

"What a guy! Every predatory female on this island had made a play for him at one time or another."

"I can understand that. He's awfully good-looking," Betty observed.

"He's cagey too. There is only one girl that I can think of that he was ever really serious about."

"You mean Miss Canton?" Betty asked.

"Well, Cheryl, of course. She's a special case. With her family's money and connection with Jack's Agency through Iwalani Shipping. I've never been quite able to figure Jack's attitude toward her. And neither has she and that's what burns her. But don't sell Cheryl short. She's got money and good looks going for her. Few men can resist that for long."

"I suppose I figured Cheryl would be the one eventually," Betty commented, though she felt it was strictly none of her business.

Again that strange feeling that had come over her in Jack's apartment assailed her. She forced it back with resolve. She had thought too much about Jack in other than business ways. That had to stop! She had better sense than to let herself get involved. No man was ever going to hurt her again, she thought stoutly. Audrey was right. No man was worth it.

"No, I didn't mean Cheryl when I spoke of another girl," said the girl. "It's one that none of us out here knows. But we've heard of her. He goes to Portland, Oregon occasionally to see her."

"I didn't know that." Betty looked at Katherine Knox wonderingly, then added, "But of course, I've only been working for him for a week."

"Long enough to fall for him," Katherine smiled.

"Not me!"

The girls returned home Sunday night, worn out but happy. The only trouble was they both overslept the next morning and were late to the office by nearly half an hour. And, as a result, all hell broke loose.

7

"**W**HERE the devil have you been?" Jack shouted when they entered.

"We went to a *hukilau* at Punaluu. Is there anything wrong with that?" Audrey retorted. She had never been afraid of Jack, or any other man for that matter.

"When you're working for me you are to report promptly. This is a business office not a play pen. The phones have been ringing off their hooks. It's all Billy and I have been able to do to keep up with it. On top of that, I had to send Warson on an errand that either of you could have handled."

"I'm sorry — " Betty began but was cut off.

"Get your book and go into my office. And you, Audrey, get on those phones. The Wahiawa branch of the Mid-Pacific bank was robbed a few minutes ago and all the news offices have been trying to get stories from us. Tell them we don't know a thing as yet. I'm waiting to hear from Bill Wilson and the police who are out there. Tell them we'll call back just as soon as we have a statement from the bank officials and the police. Got it?"

"Got it, chief," said Audrey airily. "How much loot did the bandits make off with?"

"We don't know that either. And no wise cracks, *pake*," Jack shot back, but this time his voice was edged with banter. *Pake* was the Hawaiian word for Chinaman.

Betty grabbed her book and hurried into Jack's office. She was already seated beside his desk, waiting to take dictation when he came in and closed the door rather forcibly behind him. He sat down, glared at her a moment, then his features softened.

"I tried to call you over the weekend."

Surprise leaped into her brown eyes. She looked at him not knowing what to say.

"I thought you might like to go sailing," he explained.

"I'd have loved to," Betty assured him.

"Another time, maybe?"

"He nodded. "How did you like the *hukilau*?"

"It was lots of fun."

"Where did you stay?"

"We spent the night with a friend of Audrey's. A Mrs. Knox, who had a beach house over on the other side of the island."

"I know her."

"She put us in the guest bedroom." Betty could not figure out his interest in their weekend, other than it making them late to work this morning.

"It gave you a chance to see something of the island besides Honolulu," he commented.

"Oh yes!" said Betty with sudden enthusiasm. "The drive over there was beautiful."

"Did you go over the Nuuanu Pali?" he asked.

"Something like that. Audrey got off the main highway and took me up to a look-out point."

"That's the Pali."

"We drove along a road that had bamboo and giant ferns and I don't

132

know what all growing right along side. Then we came to the look-out. Never in my whole life have I seen such a beautiful green valley. And beyond that had to be the bluest ocean in the world."

Jack smiled at her enthusiasm. "I know. I've been there many times. It's one of the more famous show places of Oahu. I guess you then went through the tunnel and up the Kam highway to Punaluu."

"It sounds right. The Kam highway I remember. It was a beautiful trip along the ocean. And then the party or *hukilau* as you call it. Gee! I never saw people have such a good time. There must have been two dozen of us. And everyone was so friendly."

"I'll bet," he said looking at her.

Betty could only marvel. Here he was, visiting with her when only a few moments ago he was furious because she and Audrey had been late for work. A strange man he was, indeed. And yet what a fascinating one. Then, suddenly, he was all business.

"Get me True Blue Wilson on the phone."

Betty stood up and started out.

"No. Stay in here. Call him from my phone."

"Who is True Blue Wilson?" She gave him a pleading look. Why couldn't he realize that she had yet to learn all of the answers around the office?"

"He's a vice president at Mid-Pac Bank." For a second he looked annoyed, then he said. "Sorry, I should have known you wouldn't know him yet." He told her the number to dial.

In a moment she was connected and asked for Mr. Wilson. A man's voice came on the phone after the transfer was made to his desk.

"Mr. Benning is calling, sir," said Betty.

"Bully for him. Put him on."

She handed Jack the receiver.

"Hi, Bill. What's the latest on the robbery?" He listened a couple of minutes while the man at the other end gave him the information. "We'll have to go with that. I'll dictate a release right away. If there is anything new on it let me know as soon as you can."

Jack hung up and told Betty to

take down the story. Then he started dictating.

"The Wahiawa branch of the Mid-Pacific Bank and Trust Company was held up five minutes after it opened this morning. A lone bandit holding a scarf over his mouth and nose and wearing dark glasses approached Dorothy Sakimoto, a teller, and threatened her with a small revolver.

"According to Miss Sakimoto, the bandit ordered her to put all the cash she had into a paper bag. When she obeyed he fled and was last seen driving away in a blue Chevrolet which appeared to be about ten years old. Miss Sakimoto screamed the instant the man was out of the bank, warning the other employees that she had just been robbed.

"Henry Hanawahine, manager of the Wahiawa branch, ran from his office, but by the time he reached the street the bandit was driving off in the car. He was unable to see the license number on the get-away auto. Police are looking for the car that Hanawahine described.

"William Wilson, senior vice president of Mid-Pacific, said the bandit made off with less than three hundred dollars. Miss Sakimoto had not yet finished setting up for the day's work at her teller's window."

"Is that all?" asked Betty, when Jack said no more.

"Yes. Type that up right away. Run off a dozen copies. Then have Billy phone the story into the news rooms."

Betty went back to her desk. She started typing at once but had to get help from Audrey as to how to spell Wahiawa, Sakimoto, and Hanawahine. Even so she completed the job, including running the copies, in less than ten minutes. She handed the copies to Billy Everett who immediately started making phone calls.

"Whew," said Betty, mostly to herself, but Audrey heard her and came over to the desk.

"Jack surely didn't take all that time to dictate a four paragraph news release," said the Chinese girl. "Did he chew you out for being late?"

"No. That's what I can't understand," Betty confessed. "He asked about the week-end. Where we stayed. What we saw and how I enjoyed the *hukilau*."

"I'll be damned," said Audrey and walked back to her desk shaking her head.

Betty could no longer ignore the interest that Jack was showing in her. In this short time it was apparent that he saw something in her that attracted his attention. She could not imagine what it might be. Her looks were not all that great she knew, especially compared to all of the gorgeous creatures here in Hawaii, both Caucasian and Oriental. Betty could not imagine her own small, though robust, body and blonde complexion attracting such a man as Jack. Audrey had suggested that might be the case, but Betty couldn't buy it. Perhaps he just felt sorry for her. Or maybe so many girls had offered themselves to him that her reserve was something of a challenge. He had no way of knowing that Lon Holderness was still in her mind, try as she had to forget him.

It was not until Betty received a newsy letter from Peg Waters several days later that Betty could even let herself take Jack seriously. In the letter Peg told her that Lon Holderness had gone to work for a company owned by his bride's family. She remembered Peg had told her that he might. Peg thought all along that Lon had married Sylvia Shaw for money. She re-read Peg's letter twice, letting the information sink in.

Slowly it came over her that Peg must have been right. Lon was after a comfortable life. He must have been more interested in that than any love he might have felt for Betty. Marrying the Shaw girl was an opportunity to make himself comfortable for life. She wondered if he had convinced the girl of his love when he asked her to marry him? Smoldering resentment began growing within her. At first it was because Lon had let her down. He had concealed his true self from her the whole time they were going together. She believed in him. But now this — ! All the time she had returned what she thought was his love, he had been looking for opportunities for himself. Her envy of Sylvia Shaw began turning into pity. What a deceitful husband she had!

It took Betty several days to adjust to this information. Part of the time she still wanted to believe Lon. The rest of the time she felt anger and bitterness over finally learning the truth. How could she ever have fallen for him, let herself get so involved that she could not see him for what he really was? She was hurt by it all, but with an entirely different reaction than she had experienced when he rejected her. Maybe now she could get him out of her system.

Perhaps now, she could find out what was in Jack's mind. Betty was quite aware that another girl, Cheryl Canton, was trying to find that out, too. Jack unwittingly threw roadblocks at them both with an announcement two days later.

"I've got to go to Portland tomorrow," he told the office force late Friday afternoon.

Betty instantly remembered what she had learned from Katherine Knox. Jack went to Portland to see a girl occasionally. Undoubtedly that's why he was going tomorrow.

"I'll be there through Monday," he continued, "then go to San Francisco where I'll be until Thursday. I'll spend the rest of the time in Los Angeles and get back here over the week-end. I'll be talking to some business men about the trade mission to Japan and seeing how many might be interested in going along. Warson and Billy, you look after the other accounts while I'm gone. I'll dictate my schedule to Betty right now. She'll make copies and give one to each of you, so you'll know where to reach me in an emergency. Get your book, Betty, and come into my office."

Betty knew that he would not be talking to business men in Portland. She wondered who the girl was, what she was like, how she looked.

In his office, Jack dictated his schedule of flights. He would be staying at the Benson Hotel in Portland and at the Clift in San Franciso. He wasn't sure yet where he'd be staying in Los Angeles but would let her know.

"And another thing. Please go through my mail every day and if there is anything urgent call me and read it," he instructed her.

"I will. Is there anything else?"

"Stay out of trouble." He glanced at her and smiled.

"Really now, did you have to say that?" Betty fluttered her long black lashes.

"Knowing you, I'd say yes."

That week-end Betty enjoyed the most relaxing two days she had had so far on the island. She wondered a time or two what Jack was doing in Portland, but put it out of her mind. Audrey went to Hilo on the Big Island Saturday morning to stay until Sunday evening. She was going to visit friends who were having a large party for some Chinese people from Taipei. Betty took advantage of her solitude to do just as she pleased without work or worry.

After a late breakfast Saturday morning, she drove to the Ala Moana shopping center. Audrey had insisted that she make use of the car over the weekend. Betty took her time exploring the apparel and accessory shops, the service centers, speciality houses, souvenir shops and acquainting herself with the large department stores such as Liberty House, Penney's and Sears.

In the afternoon she drove out to

Waikiki and took her time exploring King's Alley. She watched girls perform Hawaiian, Maori, Tahitian and Samoan island dances in a Polynesian show, went back to the Royal Hawaiian for still another look at the ocean from the colorful ocean lawn and ended with dinner at the Ship's Tavern in the Surfrider just in time to see a beautiful rainbow over Diamond Head and watch a spectacular sunset. It was the sort of day she had been needing. That night she slept better than she had the whole time she had been in Hawaii.

Sunday she went to Pearl Harbor and took the Navy launch over to the Arizona Memorial It was a moving experience and one that left her somewhat shaken. After listening to the guide explain how the ship had been sunk, she and the others who had come over on the launch were taken to the other end of the Memorial where the names of the men who were never recovered from the vessel are enshrined. A ship's bell tolled slowly. Betty had to turn away, for she felt tears welling up for those men who had died long before she was born.

Afterward, she drove up the Kamehameha Highway, through the cane and pineapple fields between the towering Koolau Range on one side and the Waianae mountains on the other. By the time she arrived at Haleiwa she decided to go on around the island, stopping at Kuillima for lunch. Though she enjoyed a sandwich while looking out over the windswept blue ocean with the drifting white clouds above her, her decision proved to be a mistake.

On Sundays the narrow Kam highway on the Windward side of Oahu is often bumper to bumper as the islanders flock to the beaches. This particular afternoon was worse than usual. The surf was up and every beach along the way had attracted surfers in droves. Toward late afternoon she found herself stalled in the traffic that crept at a snail's pace toward the Like Like and Wilson Tunnels that led through the mountain range back to Honolulu.

To make matters worse, she ran out of gas and for a hectic few minutes her car was the object of blowing horns from frustrated drivers behind her. Finally two young men came to her rescue and pushed her car in front of theirs to the nearest filling station.

"Gee, I don't know how to thank you," she told them.

"I'll tell you how. Just give us your telephone number," one of them grinned. But they were nice enough not to pursue the suggestion.

Betty dragged herself into the apartment late that evening. Audrey was already back from the Big Island.

"I was beginning to worry about you. Where have you been?" asked Audrey.

Betty told her what happened.

"I should have warned you. A Sunday traffic on the Windward Side can be brutal unless you time yourself properly. But any way you made it. So all's well that ends well. What else happened while I was gone?"

"Nothing, and I liked it that way for a change," Betty told her.

The week at Benning & Associates started in a routine way but picked up, at least for Betty, when she returned from lunch on Monday. Audrey had answered Jack's phone around one o'clock to hear

Cheryl Canton at the other end.

"She wanted to talk to him, naturally. And you should have heard the explosion when I told her he had gone to the mainland. It seems he had neglected to tell her he was going," said Audrey.

"Does he have to account to her for everything he does?"

"She'd like him to."

"Just what is their relationship?" asked Betty.

"You know as much about it as I do. There is a lot about Cheryl that a man could like. And in Jack's case there is also the Iwalani Shipping account that he has to be careful about."

"Jack wouldn't be the kind who goes after business that way," Betty remarked. For a moment she thought of Lon and what he had done to further his career.

"I don't think so either. But just the same it doesn't hurt to be tactful."

"She's beautiful. No doubt about that."

"And rich," Audrey added.

And still to be heard from, as it turned out.

A man from the Iwalani Shipping

Company called and asked for Warson Graham that afternoon. Warson was out. Betty had answered Warson's phone, since Audrey had stepped down the hall for a moment, and asked if there was anything she could do to help.

"Yes. I would like a copy of Jack's itinerary," said the man.

"I'll put a copy in the mail to you right away," she said.

"No. Give it to me over the phone," said the voice.

"Yes, sir. But if it is something we can do one of the other men in the office will be glad to handle it while Mr. Benning is gone."

"We don't need the schedule at Iwalani," said the man matter-of-factly. "Miss Canton asked me to get it for her. She's going to the mainland tonight."

Betty recovered from her astonishment, but not until the voice at the other end became insistent.

"The schedule, please."

"Yes, sir." Betty grabbed her copy and read it to him slowly so he could copy it down.

146

"Thank you," said the man and hung up.

"Oh brother!" Betty exclaimed, then turned around. Billy Everett was standing by Audrey's desk. "Want to know something? That was Iwalani Company calling. They wanted Jack's itinerary. And do you know why?"

Billy shook his head.

"Cheryl Canton asked them to get it for her."

"Why?" asked Billy.

"The man said Cheryl was going to the mainland tonight."

Audrey had come in and heard the last part of the conversation. She said, "Jack is going to have an unexpected visitor on his hands."

"I hope he doesn't get angry with me for giving out the schedule," said Betty.

"What else could you do, when Iwalani asked for it?" Bill told her. "No. He won't get sore at you. He might not like Cheryl to pop in when he's handling business for the trade mission. But he would have liked it a lot less if she had shown up in Portland over the week-end."

"Jack sees a girl there, doesn't he?"

Billy nodded.

"Do you know who she is?"

Billy shook his head. "All I know is her name. It's Helen Bader. He goes to see her three or four times a year and calls her long distance a couple of times a month."

"Sounds as if he might be serious?" Betty wondered aloud.

"Nobody has ever been able to figure out. The girl had been out here two or three times to see Jack, but he has never brought her around or introduced her to any of us. A fellow I know saw him with her one time at dinner, and said she was a most striking blonde. Older than most of the girls you see Jack with around Honolulu. But a smasher, nonetheless."

Betty caught herself feeling envious of both Helen Bader and Cheryl Canton. They both seemed to have looks, money and everything else they could want, except, perhaps, Jack. And they both had the resources to pursue him, across an ocean or anywhere else in the world. But just as quickly as that thought came to Betty she sternly forced herself to reject it. She had felt envy for Sylvia Shaw and all it had done was add to her own misery. Still it burned her that some girls had the freedom and connections to control their own destinies while others, such as she, were tossed around by the whims of fate. Oh, nonsense! she told herself. What goes on between Jack and other girls was none of her business. She was giving into her dreams like a sixteen year old.

And so she was in a receptive mood when Audrey asked her if she could be interested in going on a double date with her two days later.

"Sure, Audrey," said Betty without hesitation.

"Atta girl. The fellow I have a date with is Steve Fong. He's being visited by an old college roommate who lived in Hong Kong. He showed up rather unexpectedly and Steve wants to make it a foursome tonight, rather than just me and the two guys."

"Sounds interesting." Betty had never dated a Chinese boy before and looked forward to the experience.

Her date, Charlie Kwak, turned out

to be a nice looking, highly-educated young man who flattered Betty all evening with his attention and concern for her happiness and pleasure. He was the son of a wealthy Hong Kong banker and described the wonders of Kowloon, Victoria and other areas of the famous British Crown Colony where he had grown up in a manner that would have done credit to the most ardent chamber of commerce member.

The four of them had cocktails on the ocean lawn of the Halekulani, under the banyan tree while a trio sang songs of the islands. A gentle breeze blew in over the Koolau Range causing the Royal palms to sway and nod lazily.

Afterward they went to the House of Hong, a second floor restaurant on a side street in Waikiki. Betty had eaten Chinese food before, but she never had eaten anything like the dinner Steve and Charlie ordered. It started off with another cocktail. Then came, in succession, chicken sweet corn soup, mushrooms and Chinese greens, fried won ton, sweet and sour pork, shredded beef with bamboo shoots, fried rice Hong

Kong style and on and on until Betty's stomach felt as though it would burst. If all this didn't result in indigestion she'd be one surprised blonde.

"I simply can't eat another bite," she announced abruptly.

"You did very well," Charlie complimented. "But in a few hours you will be hungry again."

"Want to bet?" Betty smiled and sat back in her chair, feeling like an overstuffed buddha.

"That's how it is with Chinese cooking. How about a little more oolong and a fortune cookie?"

"Tea yes. Cookie no!" Betty laughed.

"When you come to visit in Hong Kong, I'll see that you get plenty to eat. Are you coming soon?" asked Charlie.

"Nothing she does would surprise me," Audrey spoke up. "She sure hit Oahu with a bang." And she related the story about Jack's Thunderbird and the fire hydrant.

"I remember seeing that picture on the front page of the newspaper a few weeks ago. Was that you?" Steve Fong looked at Betty admiringly.

"Unfortunately, yes," she admitted.

"Hey, Charlie. You have a date with a celebrity tonight. How about that!" Steve laughed.

"I knew that all along," said the young man from Hong Kong. "And now I insist that you come to Hong Kong and let me show you that part of the world."

"My chances of getting to Hong Kong are about the same as getting to the moon," said Betty.

Then suddenly she was silent, pondering her own words. Only a month ago she would have said the same thing about Hawaii. She was beginning to learn that one can never be sure of what might happen, what strange set of events might conspire to alter a person's life. The ingredients were usually there, but seldom were they recognized.

"I take it all back," she amended. "Maybe I will get to Hong Kong sometime."

And that night when Betty and Audrey were back in the apartment getting ready for bed, the Chinese girl made an observation.

"I saw how you worked on Charlie

152

Kwak toward the last. I tell you, you underestimate yourself, gal."

Betty was not sure that Audrey was right, but the girl did wonders for her ego when she talked like that. Her tragic affair back in St. Louis had undermined her self-confidence and caused her to retire behind a facade of aloofness. She realized that she was gradually getting rid of that attitude as if she was returning to the land of the living.

And her attitude toward others was changing. Cheryl Canton could fly to the mainland. Helen Bader could call from Portland. They could reach Jack at their whim. What neither of them could do was be with him as his secretary day after day in the office. If those and other girls thought she was a threat, maybe Betty could give them real reasons for thinking so. She smiled to herself at the thought.

Jack returned to the office the following Monday as he had planned. He was excited about his success in promoting interest in the trade mission. It looked as if the event would take off about a month from now. There was still a great

153

amount of work to be done, but, in a pep talk to his associates, he assured them that if they all pitched in the enterprise would be a success. And the associates of the Benning agency would be properly rewarded.

"Did Miss Canton contact you on the mainland?" Betty asked him when she got a moment alone with him in his office.

"Why, yes. How did you know?" He looked at her with surprise.

"She had someone at Iwalani call for your schedule."

"Hummmm." Jack's dark eyes stared out of the window for a moment, thinking. When he turned back he shrugged. "Cheryl usually gets what she wants."

And with that remark he suddenly became all business. He dictated some letters, among which was one to Mr. Placer. He told Betty's former boss about the trade mission and suggested that the Placer Agency see if anyone in the midwest would be interested in trying to drum up some business or financial backing in Japan. Then he gave orders to

Billy Everett to start work on pamphlets and display racks that would comprise the trade exhibit that would be taken along to Japan.

Betty found herself with a growing interest in the project. She had never worked on anything like it before. She began making notes on her own as to what all was involved. Within a week, Jack had twelve men representing banks, oil, steel, shipping, utilities and other interests definitely signed up for the trip and several more were showing great interest. All these matters Betty noted in her journal, along with helpful information about addresses, telephone numbers, schedule and deadlines.

One day Jack called her in and began dictating a long check list of items needed toward final organization of the trade mission. He had been dictating only a few minutes before Betty realized that she had already assembled most of this material in her journal.

"I think I have most of this written down," she interrupted.

"What do you mean?" he stared at her, puzzled.

"Wait a minute."

She hurried out to her desk and came back with several stapled sheets of paper. She handed it to Jack.

"That's what I mean."

He looked it over quickly. The surprise on his face turned to approval, then admiration. Quickly he read it through. Betty had been right. With few exceptions, she had documented the things he had wanted to dictate.

"Great. This will save me a lot of time and worry. Will you keep a diary from now on? I'll think of things to put in it along with what you and Billy come up with. How on earth did you think of doing this, Betty?" he asked, looking her over, as if he had not really seen her before.

Maybe it had been a subconscious act on her part. She didn't really know. But when he asked her the question she immediately knew the answer. And she had known it, without admitting it, all along.

"Because," she said looking at him levelly, "I want to go with you to Japan."

8

BETTY sniffed the exotic odor of jasmine as a pretty little Filipino girl held out to her a small vial of pikake perfume. She tried, in turn, the fragrances of Wicked Wahine and Royal Lei. The clerk, who provided her own special splash of color and beauty, smiled at her.

"You like?"

"I like them all," said Betty, standing undecided at the perfume counter in a store on the Fort Street Mall in downtown Honolulu.

It was three days since she had made the pitch to Jack about going to Japan with the trade mission. She had advanced the argument that she wanted to go because she could contribute something to the junket. She could help him as his secretary by relieving him of a good many details to look after. And she could act as a sort of secretary to the whole group in whatever way was required.

157

"No doubt, what you say is true," Jack agreed, but still he did not say she could go. He looked pensive.

"Is there a possibility you might take me?"

"I don't know."

"Will you consider it?"

"Yes."

"Well — ?"

Her eyes were questioning, trying to see into his but he avoided looking at her. If there was such a thing as willing an event to take place, Betty thought at that moment it would surely make him decide. Every ounce of her awareness concentrated on getting him to make a favorable decision. She was tense, hopeful and silently urging him on.

"I'll have to think it over," he said finally, breaking the spell. Betty swallowed her immediate disappointment, but took heart that his response had not been negative.

If he had been thinking it over he had given her no inkling for the past three days. He had immediately gotten busy and nothing more had been said. She had been afraid to push him any harder.

It might cause him to over-react against the idea and tell her bluntly and with finality that she could not go.

Her purpose in trying out some perfume was, she told herself, silly. But her instinct had persuaded her otherwise. She hoped it might make him more aware of her, if that's what was needed. Anyway, it was worth a try. She had intended buying some Hawaiian perfume before now, but had not gotten around to it. She would not have done it this morning, either, had not Jack sent her to the State Capitol building with a package of material about the trade mission for an official in the Department of Commerce.

After making the delivery she was to meet Jack, Billy and a representative of Japanese Air Lines at the Press Club for lunch. Having a few minutes to spare, she had walked from the Capitol into downtown Honolulu and looked around in a part of the city that she had never seen before.

"I'll take this one," said Betty to the clerk and indicated the pikake perfume.

"That's a very good one," the girl assured her.

After the purchase, Betty sauntered along the mall until she came to King Street. The Honolulu Press Club was located somewhere near, according to the directions Billy had given her. She glanced at a street number and headed west for two blocks until she found the address.

It was an old two-story brick building that had undergone extensive renovation and modernization. She glanced further up the street and noticed that the whole area seemed to be undergoing a face lifting. She entered the building and walked up wide winding stairs to the second floor. The Press Club was identified by a carved wooden sign over a heavy wooden door.

Inside she saw an attractive room with deliberately unfinished brick walls that gave it a quaint appearance. The only wall decorations were line drawing caricatures of some of the members. A large bar stretched across one corner of the room and the rest of the space was filled with tables and chairs that were set

160

up for the lunch-time trade.

Betty was still a bit early and the only people in the Club were two waitresses and three men who were standing at the bar.

"Mr. Benning made a reservation for four of us for lunch," Betty told the waitress who came over to help her.

"Right over here. We're holding this table for him. Would you care to sit down and have something from the bar while you wait?"

"No thank you," said Betty.

"How've you been?" came a man's voice at that moment. Betty looked around and saw Nick Lyons, the young man who had taken her to dinner at Diamond Head a few weeks ago. He was standing at the bar with two companions.

"Hello, Nick," she smiled.

He came over to the table. "What are you doing here? Alone, I hope, so I can have you to myself for lunch."

"No way. I'm to meet Jack and Billy and a man from the Japan Air Lines. I had to come on into town on an errand which got me here a bit early. How've you been, Nick?" she asked pleasantly.

"I've been missing you."

"Well, give me a ring sometime," she smiled.

"I tried once. Called the office. You were out but I got Jack instead. When I told him I wanted to talk with you he asked me what for. And I got the notion that he didn't like it when I said I wanted a date."

"You could have called back."

"I've forgotten why I didn't, something came up. But you can be sure I will. What's Jack cooking up these days?"

"We're all working like mad on the trade mission."

"I've heard about that. Sounds great — "

Just then the door to the Club opened and Jack came in followed by Billy and a small Japanese man carrying a brief case. They came to the table and Betty was introduced to Mr. Kiyoo Maruyama, a local representative of the Japanese Air line.

"Hello, Jack," said Nick.

"Hi," Jack replied. He seemed somewhat annoyed.

"Why is it every time I want to talk

with Betty I end up with you?" Nick smiled.

"Somebody has to shoo away the wolves."

With a cheerful wave, Nick went back to the bar and the three men sat down at the table with Betty. Jack looked at her, then toward Nick, then back to her again.

"He still after a date?"

"Yes."

"Remember what I told you about him."

He said no more about Nick. To the waitress he said they all would have cocktails, then gave her their order. The men had martinis but Betty asked for tomato juice. She ordered a grilled sandwich when the waitress asked what they wished for lunch. With that out of the way, the men began discussing the trade mission trip to Japan and Betty made notes as they went along.

"You can be sure Japan Air Lines will do everything possible to make the trip comfortable and pleasant. We have ways of adding to some of the amenities for special groups," said Mr. Maruyama.

"Such as?" asked Jack.

"It will be a bit more expensive but it would be nice if you could be in the forward lounge. That's where we can provide you with special food and drink. We could even put on a special hostess to look after your party."

They discussed prices. For round trip fare, Jack estimated they could take advantage of the service Maruyama suggested. After all, the party would be composed of business men, most of whom could afford such amenities. If not, their companies could. Most of them would be on expense accounts.

"We could block out the whole first class compartment," Maruyama explained.

"How many would it accommodate?" asked Jack.

"Forty. Twenty seats on each side."

"Our group will be composed of about twenty."

"No problem. We could put you all on one side, or the first five rows on each side. Do you know exactly how many are going?"

"Not yet." Jack turned to Billy.

"What's the count so far?"

"Sixteen men and three wives, I think." Billy got out the list of those who signed up. He looked it over then nodded. "That's right. Nineteen so far."

"I think you're wrong. It should be twenty," said Jack.

Billy frowned. He rechecked the list. "No. I'm right. Nineteen. And that includes you and me."

"Let me see that." Jack took the list and looked it over quickly. "It's twenty, as I said. You haven't included Betty."

Betty had been about to take a bite of her sandwich when Jack made that remark. She stopped, her mouth open and the sandwich held in the air. Her startled eyes looked at Jack.

"I didn't know she was going," said Billy.

"Well, she is."

Billy added Betty's name to the list then glanced at her and smiled.

Betty put down her sandwich. She could hardly believe what she had heard. She stared at Jack. When had he decided that? And why hadn't he told her? She wondered if she would ever learn to understand him? She was about to thank him profusely, but by then the men were already discussing further arrangements. Betty's mind was in disarray as she tried to keep up with her notes. She couldn't get over what she had heard, and just couldn't understand the offhanded way she had learned of it. Going to Japan? Think of that!

"I didn't get a chance to thank you during lunch, but I sure want to thank you now for putting my name on that list," said Betty as she and Jack and Billy rode back to the office.

"We need you along with us, don't we Billy?" said Jack.

"Sure," Billy agreed instantly.

"When did you decide to take me along?" she asked. Curiosity had gotten the better of her and she simply had to find that out.

"I don't know. What difference does it make?"

"Oh, none at all. It's just that I'm overwhelmed. I promise both of you that I'll really work hard. I'll earn my way."

When they were back in the office, Billy came to her desk and congratulated her. He was glad she was going. He said Betty could be of great help to both him and Jack in handling some of the details.

"That's what I told Jack the other day," she replied.

"Oh? You talked to him about going along?"

"I asked him if I could."

"Well," he laughed. "You made it."

"Made what?" Audrey asked from her desk.

"I'm going to Japan with the trade mission."

"Wow!" Audrey exclaimed. "How'd you work that?"

"I'll never know," said Betty truthfully.

She plunged even harder into the work of getting ready. There were personal considerations that she hadn't thought of. Billy pointed out that she had to get a passport, if she didn't already have one. And she had to get an international certificate of vaccination.

"How in the world do I go about getting all of that?" she asked Billy.

"Call the passport service, dumdumb," he cracked.

"Well, how was I supposed to know?" she complained.

Betty did as she was told and found out, to her horror, that she had to have a birth certificate. She fired off a letter to the City Hall in St. Louis requesting a copy of her birth certificate by return mail, if possible. Also, she had to have an identification photograph to the specification of two and a half by two and a half inches, in black and white or color. That was no problem. Benning & Associates had connections with several commercial photographers. Betty got a picture of herself for passport purposes within three days. The birth certificate arrived a week later.

Jack let her take an extra hour during her lunch period and, with the required information, she went to the Federal Building in downtown Honolulu. After she had filled out a form and given the clerk the picture and certificate, she had to pay thirteen dollars and then was told that her passport would be ready in three or four days.

Later that same day, she went to a doctor's office down the hall from

Benning & Associates and received her vaccination. Audrey had arranged that through a girl she knew who worked in the doctor's office. It didn't hurt and it didn't make her sick, but she had to wear a band aid on her upper arm. And when that was removed an unattractive scar remained visible on her arm for another week.

"Whew," she told Audrey one night when they were in the apartment. "I had no idea so much was involved in order to get to Japan."

"Have you thought about needing more clothes?"

"No. Won't what I wear here do out there?"

"Not unless you have something heavier than Hawaiian wear. It's nice weather in Japan in the springtime, but you'll run into some days that are cold and damp."

Betty reviewed her wardrobe and decided on buying another pants suit and a long dress. That should do it. She did her shopping in the evenings and recruited Audrey to help during the few evenings she didn't have a date.

But her own problems were insignificant compared to the preparations that were going forward at Benning & Associates. It became necessary for the entire office staff to put in evening hours. Billy was being inundated with brochures, maps and other types of printed and photographic information that various members of the mission wanted included in the exhibit. Warson and Audrey, along with Billy and Betty, began spending evenings at the office. And, as time went on and the departure date came closer, Jack himself began staying late.

Betty did not begrudge a single minute of the extra time she spent in the office. It was stimulating work. She enjoyed the later hours, especially when they all delayed dinner until they were finished and went together to some good restaurant. Jack usually was along and in a relaxed mood, knowing that his employees were turning in first-class team work. He would insist they all join him for cocktails followed by a good steak or whatever they might choose.

But there was someone else who did resent those evenings and the fact that

Betty was going to Japan. When Cheryl found out about it she expressed herself in explicitly and colorful language at the Iwalani Shipping Company. Warson Graham, who was handling the Iwalani account for the time being found out about it through the shipping company grapevine. He was a discreet man and kept it to himself. But a remark he dropped one day in the presence of Audrey caused her to birddog for more information. She pumped Warson and made inquiries through connections of her own at Iwalani.

"Cheryl's furious, especially because Jack is taking you on the trade mission," she told Betty.

"I figured she would be when she found out about it," Betty replied.

"Hell hath no fury, you know," Audrey quoted.

"I'm not sure but what that has always been a half-baked saying." Betty had never reacted with fury in her case with Lon Holderness back in St. Louis.

"Don't take it for granted when it comes to Cheryl. I wouldn't put anything past her. Iwalani is a good account for Benning & Associates. And she has plenty of clout as a stockholder in that company, even though top management is composed of outside-the-family professionals."

Late one evening the office force was relaxing over dinner at Chez Michel, a charming French restaurant on Kalakaua Avenue in the Waikiki district. Jack and Mike Martin, the owner and operator, were old friends and tonight Mike was outdoing himself with excellent food, efficient waiters and delightful wine. Betty had breast of Ewa chicken done in a white wine sauce which she declared to be the best chicken she had ever eaten. Pleased, Mike poured another glass of Grey Reisling wine. Everyone was in a good mood, happy with the work they had accomplished that evening. Jack was especially pleased and showed it by complimenting everyone and particularly Betty who sat on his right.

Into this convivial melange came Cheryl Canton with two gentlemen friends. Martin made the mistake of giving them a table right next to where the jolly crew of Benning & Associates were holding forth. Betty was the first to notice her.

"Oh oh," she said under her breath.

"What did you say?" Jack leaned toward her.

Just then he saw Cheryl. She was eyeing him venomously, her lips a thin line of anger and disapproval. If Jack was taken aback he didn't show it. He called to Cheryl and waved to her, then seeing her two companions he called to them both, using their first names. When the three were seated he got up and went to their table.

"How's it going, Jack? I've heard about the trade mission you're organizing," said one of the men.

"We're working like dogs. Day and night. Departure time is less than three weeks away. I've been tied up almost every night."

"Do you think I don't know that!" Cheryl fumed.

Everyone at the Benning table had quieted down and it was impossible not to hear the exchange.

"I'm sorry, darling," said Jack, giving her a smile calculated to charm the worst jury into a favorable verdict, but I really have been busy."

"So I see!" Cheryl cast a glance of disillusionment toward Betty and the others.

"But I really have," Jack insisted. "Everyone involved wants the mission to be a success. There's a lot riding on it, you know."

"How well I know!" Cheryl was not about to give in.

"Then be patient. As we get closer to departure, I'll have more time. Believe that or not. And I intend to see as much of you as I can before we go."

"Why that, all of a sudden?" she demanded.

His smile continued but now his eyes had the look of a man long denied and one who could hardly wait to get with his lady love. Cheryl must have been a bit mollified, but she returned his peace offering with sarcasm.

"I can hardly wait."

Betty watched this performance with mixed feelings. Jack was quite openly solicitous of the brunette's good will. She wondered just how sincere he was

174

and how meaningful the look with which he favored the girl. Jack sent a waiter for drinks for Cheryl and her companions, then returned to his chair beside Betty.

"Well, kids, how are you all feeling? I want you all to get a good night's rest so we can get back at it early in the morning. Did everyone get enough to eat?"

It was hard to say if Jack was sounding a little too jolly. He was walking a tightrope. No doubt of that. But his easy manner belied any nervousness that he may be feeling. Betty did not know how much of a show he was putting on for Cheryl's benefit but he was handling the matter without once showing concern.

"I'll say one thing for him," Audrey commented when they were alone in the apartment and getting ready for bed, "Jack Benning can make any girl feel as if she is the only one in his life. I often wonder just how many have ever fallen for him."

Well, Betty told herself, she was one who had begun to fall for him. And maybe it was time that she put on the brakes. She realized that she had been slipping into that frame of mind for some time. He had made it so easy for her. Was there danger in it? More hurt? More heartbreak?

Long after Audrey had gone to sleep, Betty lay awake staring up into the darkness. She wanted to trust Jack. But any man who could handle a difficult situation such as he had faced this evening might be capable of other deceptions.

Betty wished she had not gone to Chez Michel's this evening. It had given her too much to think about. She tried to get to sleep, but could not. Too many thoughts crowded into her mind, thoughts laced with doubt and uncertainty. Jack had made no effort to conceal his interest in her, but was that, too, a deception? Her heart felt a sudden chill at the thought. Finally she told herself sternly that such speculation had to stop. She was going to Japan. She was going with Jack. Surely, she could find out the truth about him on such a trip.

The stars were high and wan in the Hawaiian night when she finally dropped off to sleep.

9

"WHERE'S Jack?"

It was not the words that brought Betty to attention one afternoon several days later, it was the husky, slightly accented feminine voice. Betty looked around as the girl burst into the office. She made her presence felt instantly by giving everyone a dazzling smile. Audrey looked at her wide-eyed. Billy glanced up from a stack of material on his desk, did a double-take, then stared fascinated. Warson missed out, for he had left earlier that afternoon.

"He's not in," said Betty, looking at the girl wonderingly.

Her exquisite yet robust build was covered by a sensational navy blue pants suit with wide open collar that revealed flawless ivory skin. She had a short nose, high cheek bones and straight blonde hair that was combed back smoothly into a chignon at the back of her well-shaped head. Her red mouth was full and sensuous. Her large dark eyes were covered by enormous tinted glasses. She seemed to be somewhat older, in her thirties perhaps. It was hard to tell because of the feeling of excitement that she generated.

"I'll wait," and before Betty could tell her that Jack was gone for the day, she introduced herself to one and all. "I'm Helen Bader. And how lovely it is to be back in the Islands. My, how things have changed since first I was here! I was a little girl. Can you imagine?"

"Mr. Benning will not be in again until the morning," said Betty.

"Then where can we reach him? I must let him know I'm here. My time is very limited."

"He's with a client. Possibly you could reach him at his apartment this evening."

"Can we call the client?" her tone was not insistent. It was honest inquiry.

"I — I doubt if he wants to be disturbed," said Betty, hesitantly. She knew he was at the office of the Land and Development Company, trying to get some matters cleared with them, before the trip to Japan.

"Do you think it would disturb him to learn I'm in town?" Helen Bader gave a hearty laugh.

"Oh, no, I didn't mean in that way — " Betty began, but the girl cut in.

"You could be right. Business before pleasure. Let's not bother him. I'll leave word at his apartment to have him call me. I'll be at the Kahala Hilton for two days. Then I'm off to New Zealand for some skiing. Have any of you ever been there?"

They shook their heads and looked at her in awe, not because she was going to New Zealand, but because she was the sort of person who, somehow, demanded attention.

"I was only there once," she went on. "It's such a lovely country and so very remote. Makes you feel as if you were at the end of the earth, which you are since the next stop is Antarctica. I hope all of you can go there sometime. Will you?"

She fixed her eyes on Betty who was momentarily at a loss for words. "I — I don't know," she recovered and added. "First, I'm going to Japan."

"Are you really? When?" Helen Bader looked at her with genuine interest.

"I'm going with the trade mission that Mr. Benning is organizing."

"How awfully nice for you. Will it be your first journey to the Far East?"

"Yes."

"And how about the others?" The blonde turned and gathered Billy and Audrey into the conversation. "Are you all going?"

"I am," said Billy.

"And I'm staying home. Someone has to mind the store," Audrey said laconically.

"Well, it will be your turn next time," said the blonde, favoring the Chinese girl with a reassuring smile. "Everything happens for the best. By staying home you might suddenly strike it rich. Who can tell?" And the tone of voice she used while saying it made it seem a distinct possibility.

"If Mr. Benning calls in, I'll tell him you were here," Betty volunteered.

"Thank you so very much. I appreciate that and so will Jack. I could not pass up seeing him even though my time is very short. I hate to go to places and see people when there is too little time to enjoy their company. Life is too short for all of us, isn't it? Makes it difficult to assign the right priorities. What one wants most to do, I mean."

"You sound as if you do pretty much as you wish," Audrey smiled, having recovered from the initial feeling of intimidation she had felt in Helen Bader's presence.

"I do? Why do you say that?"

"Well — " suddenly Audrey found herself searching for an explanation of something she had thought would not need one. "You look as if you enjoy yourself."

"Really? Why shouldn't I? Why shouldn't everyone? I have fun and I love life. And isn't that what it's all about?" she said good-naturedly.

They agreed with her.

"Never have hang-ups. I'm a cross between Pavlova and Gypsy Rose Lee but it's never bothered me. I would rather have been one or the other, but that's what comes of being a split personality. And hasn't it been nice to enjoy the best of two lives?" Suddenly she apologized. "But I'm taking up too much of your time. I'm sure you will have much to get done before the office closes. It was so nice meeting you all. Aloha, until we meet again."

And with that, Helen Bader swept out of the office leaving three employees of Benning & Associates looking at each other. Billy was the first to speak.

"Did that really happen? Did we really have a girl like that visiting us?" he said, thinking out loud.

"Who do you suppose she is?" asked Audrey.

"She must be the one he sees in Portland," Betty guessed.

"Golly! If she can talk that much in ten minutes with people she has never met before, what would she do visiting with someone for the evening?"

"Don't you know, Audrey?" Billy leered.

Shortly before five o'clock, Betty received a call from Jack. He wanted to know if there were any messages.

"Yes. A girl by the name of Helen Bader came in."

"Helen is in town?" Jack exclaimed, his voice betraying his surprise.

"She's staying at the Kahala Hilton."

"I'll call her right away." He hung up immediately.

Betty wondered what affect the unexpected visit of the blonde bombshell would have on Jack. It was certainly putting Betty in her place. She was still wondering about it two days later. The office had seen very little of him until after his return from the airport where, undoubtedly, he had put Helen Bader on the plane to New Zealand.

He said nothing at all about the girl when he returned to the office; just plunged into the work that had piled up on his desk.

Maybe someday, Betty decided, she would learn what Helen Bader meant to Jack, just as someday she might find out the same thing about Cheryl Canton. What chance would a mere secretary have against two such overwhelming girls as Helen and Cheryl, Betty reflected moodily.

But during the next two weeks there was little time for Betty to reflect on

183

anything but getting ready for the trip to Japan. Twenty-three persons were signed up to go, representing a divergent group of business men. All had two things in common. They were interested in promoting trade with Japan and in getting Japanese money invested in their businesses.

The displays that Billy had been working on were now in the construction stage and Jack was pushing to get them finished so they could be set up and looked over before being again disassembled and shipped to Japan. Along with that were going hundreds of pieces of printed material, brochures and photographic presentations.

Betty's job, among other things, was to catalogue every piece of material so that it could be accounted for when they arrived in Tokyo. She managed it with hard work and efficiency while at the same time keeping a daily progress record in her journal for Jack to use as a check list. And then there was necessary dictation to take from him on routine office matters. After all, Benning & Associates could not ignore its other clients while preparing for a trip to the Orient.

It was a great lesson in organization; one Betty would not forget. She began to think of Jack as a genius. Not many business men could have gotten such cooperation from their employees and handled their clients so considerately that none of them thought they were being neglected.

She found herself adding one more accolade to her assessment of him. Admiration. This was an objective assessment whereas her others were more nearly products of her emotional reaction to him. She knew enough about the business world and public relations to recognize an expert when she saw one, albeit an unpredictable one. He got things done. She was proud of her boss. And she was proud to be a part of his team.

Sometimes she wondered if he appreciated her work. He had said very little to her lately in the way of a compliment about her efforts. And so she was in a frame of mind to accept a dinner invitation from Nick Lyons when he called late one afternoon.

He took her to the Outrigger Canoe Club, a private dining club in a beautiful setting at Diamond head, where they could look out at the sunset at cocktail time. Pink clouds were drifting over a darkening ocean and white sails were harbor bound for the night.

They had just put in their dinner orders when Nick nodded toward the entrance. Betty followed the direction of his glance and saw Cheryl and Jack entering.

"I see your boss and his boss are with us tonight," said Nick.

"What do you mean, his boss?" Betty asked.

"Anyone who has anything to do with Iwalani Shipping had better take Cheryl into account. And Iwalani is one of Jack's better clients. He represents them in a public relations way and also does some work for them in industrial relations."

"I know that," Betty responded a bit crisply.

"Then you also know what I mean about Cheryl Canton."

"I know nothing about Jack's relationship with Cheryl or Helen Bader or anyone else," she assured him.

"Helen who?" Nick's interest was suddenly aroused.

"Helen Bader."

Betty glanced at him. Perhaps Nick knew the girl, and she might have an opportunity to find out about her. She waited expectantly. He pondered a moment then shook his head.

"At first the name seemed to ring a bell. But I guess I was thinking of two other people."

"She was here not so long ago, on her way to New Zealand," Betty added hoping to jog his memory.

"No. It couldn't be," he said.

At that point, Jack saw them and waved. They sat at a table on the other side of the room. Betty was glad they had not been shown to a table close to her and Nick. Not that she felt completely out of it this evening. She had on a new long dress that she had bought to take along to Japan for the reception that was to be held at the Tokyo-America Club. She could never present the startling good looks that Cheryl always had, but at least she could be well dressed.

"Jack is no fool, Betty. I'm sure you know that," said Nick.

"Of course he isn't. But do you think he's interested in Cheryl only because of her money?" She sounded somewhat defensive because the very thought of it aroused anguish in her heart.

"No." Suddenly Nick looked at her earnestly. "Anyway, why worry about them? I'm worried about missing you, while you're in Japan."

"You've been kind to me, Nick, and I appreciate it. I'll miss you too."

She meant it. Nick was the sort of man she felt comfortable with. He had replaced her loneliness with companionship, at least a little. But she knew that she could never take him seriously.

The following morning in the privacy of his office, Jack again reminded Betty that Nick Lyons was married, even though he might be trying to get a divorce. He warned her not to get involved with him.

"I don't think you have to warn me of that a second time," she said, unable to hide the defiance in her voice. "I remember what you said. But I see no harm in having a date with him occasionally. My time is my own when I'm not in the office, isn't it?"

Their eyes locked. She saw in his anger and frustration. Her own feeling suddenly became understandable to her. Jack had no right to lecture her. After all, he did not hesitate to date whoever he pleased. Theirs was a working relationship. It had nothing to do with their private lives. She kept telling herself that over and over, as if drilling it into her own head was the only way she could believe it.

"Yes, of course," said Jack tonelessly. Then he turned to business. "I've got the Four-A suite at the Ilikai for a sendoff party for everyone who is going on the trade mission. I want you to see that all arrangements are made. It will be held the evening before our departure. Will you handle it?"

"Certainly." Betty glanced at her calendar when she returned to her desk. The party would be next Monday evening. She could hardly believe that in less than five days she would board a plane headed for Japan. But her mind dwelt on that for only a moment. There were a hundred details to be handled between now and departure.

Everyone at Benning & Associates, with the exception of Jack, worked over the weekend. Billy was working himself into a nervous breakdown over problems of packaging and transportation and he needed all the help he could get. Betty spent Saturday morning at the Ilikai checking out arrangements for the party Monday night, then returned to the office and pitched in. Sunday night was the only time she had in which to do her own packing.

Late Monday afternoon, Betty and Audrey hurried to the apartment and changed into long dresses. Betty wore a white and black print with matching cardigan jacket and the Chinese girl put on an oriental poppy printed dress with a Mandarin collar. Then they went to the hotel to the Four-A suite that looked out over the Marina and the ocean. A wide choice of pupus had been set up on one side of the giant picture window. In the opposite corner was a small bar. A waitress and bartender were on hand.

Billy and Warson arrived shortly and gave everyone name tags, identifying them as representatives of Benning & Associates. Mr. Maruyama, the Japan Air Lines representative, came in next. The last to arrive was Jack, dressed in an attractive double breasted maroon jacket with brass buttons, white trousers and white shoes.

"All present and accounted for, I see. Good work, kids. I'll introduce you to the trade mission people as they arrive. Audrey, you and Betty look after the three wives who are going along. Put them at ease, if they aren't already. I wish we were all going on the trip tomorrow, but a couple of you can't be spared from the office." Jack smiled at Audrey and Warson.

A moment later the first three guests arrived. It was an auspicious beginning. They were business men accustomed to meeting people and in no time were on congenial terms, especially with Betty and Audrey. The other guests began arriving and Betty, who had looked at all their names many times on the list, did her best to remember what name went with whom as she met them. When everyone was there, Jack asked for their attention for just five minutes; then they could get back to the drinks and the pupus.

"By now I'm sure you've met all the Benning people, but I want to introduce them again. Warson Graham and Audrey Ching will not be with us on the trip. They will look after other accounts while we're gone. Billy Everett will be in charge of setting up the exhibits at the Trade Center in Tokyo. And last, Betty Lane, my secretary, will be the girl Friday to all of you. Anything she can do to make the trip pleasant and a success, don't hesitate to ask her."

"I think she's going to make a trip a success just by being on it," one of the men spoke up. "And I think Miss Ching should come along too."

"How about that, Jack?" Audrey exclaimed, laughing.

It was a congenial group of people who were going on the trip and Betty had enjoyed meeting them all. Around eight o'clock the party began thinning out. All were to be at the airport at ten thirty in the morning, an hour before departure time.

Betty and Billy were there at nine o'clock, checking over last minute details with Mr. Maruyama. All the exhibit material was accounted for and had been turned over to the Japan Air Lines for shipment. Maruyama would see to it that all the luggage belonging to the trade mission people would be properly labeled and loaded. In Japan special arrangements had been made for the members to clear customs as a group and their luggage delivered to the New Otani hotel in Tokyo.

By a quarter to eleven all members of the group had checked in. At that point Mr. Maruyama took charge. He led the party through the lounge to a special area and announced that all members of the trade mission would be taken aboard the aircraft in just a few minutes, in advance of the regular passengers.

Betty was taken ahead of everyone, for she had the list of trade mission members. She was introduced to a small, exquisite Japanese girl in a kimono decorated with white spider mums like fireworks against a midnight blue background.

"Miss Rane? she asked.

"Lane," Betty corrected, then remembered that some Japanese had trouble with the letter 'L' "but Rane will do," she laughed.

"We'rcome to Japan Air Rines Garden Jet," the little hostess bowed. "When your guests come aboard, prease to introduce me. My name is Kazuka and I am your special hostess for you."

"*Domo arigato gozaimasu*." 'Thank you very much,' said Betty.

"Ahsooo, you speak Japanese."

"*Sukoshi*," 'a little,' Betty replied.

The front lounge of the aircraft was beautifully decorated with Japanese designs and seemed more like an elegant living room. Kazuko showed Betty up a spiral stair to the tea house in the sky where cocktails would be served. And then, all at once, the party began to arrive. Betty helped Kazuko direct them to their assigned seats. Then Billy and Jack came aboard, followed by Maruyama.

"Welcome to flight number seventy-one," Betty smiled.

"Looks as if you've done a good job,"

Jack complimented her as he glanced up the aisle, pleased that everyone had been shown to their seats without mix-up.

"Thanks, but it's a miracle that everything worked out. I've never done anything like this before," said Betty, relieved.

Shortly, the regular passengers began boarding. Kazuko was assisted in the forward lounge by two other Japanese hostesses and a flight steward who began making everyone comfortable, answering questions and handing out menus for lunch. Flight time to Tokyo was announced at approximately nine hours. However, it would be three o'clock Tokyo time when they arrived, the difference being the hours' difference in Tokyo and Honolulu time. And, because they would be crossing the international dateline, there would be a day's difference.

Betty found all of this somewhat confusing, even though she had tried to digest the information earlier when working on the trip. And to add to her confusion, she reminded herself that according to Honolulu time they would arrive in Tokyo around eight o'clock in the evening. One of the wives asked her about this very point, and all Betty could do was to add to the lady's confusion.

"This is my first trip to Japan, too," Betty confessed.

"Really? From the way you've been handling matters, I assumed you had done this many times," said the woman whose name was Louise Leyhe. Her husband, Fred, represented a timber company in Oregon. "Anyway, I think you are a very efficient young lady, and a pretty one too. I am looking forward to getting to know you better during the trip."

"Thank you," said Betty, just as the intercom came on and instructed everyone to go to their seats and fasten seat belts prior to take-off.

Three seats had been assigned to the Benning & Associates personnel. Billy was already in the window seat so Betty sat down beside him. Jack came along a moment later, looked at her, then sat down in the seat directly ahead. A seductive Japanese girl's voice came on the intercom and welcomed all passengers in English to Japan Air Lines flight Seventy-one whose destination was Tokyo International Airport. She made a few announcements about safety, then gave the same information in Japanese.

The great plane moved out onto the runway. In a few moments the engines were revved up and the aircraft took off. Betty caught a glimpse of Honolulu and Diamond Head as the plane circled ever higher, then headed west toward the Far East.

"Think of it!" she exclaimed, mainly to herself but Billy looked around at her questioningly. She added hastily. "We're on our way to Japan."

"Well, of course. After all I've been through getting ready for this, I'd hate to end up in Belgium," he said in a tired voice.

In a few minutes the seat belt sign was turned off. Jack immediately unfastened his and stood up. He turned around to Betty.

"Come with me," he said.

She unfastened her seat belt and followed him, having no idea where he was taking her or why. He led the way up the small winding stairs to the tea-house-in-the-sky lounge above.

"Isn't this better?" he sat down and indicated the seat next to him.

"Why — yes. It's nice up here. The hostess showed me this place before we began boarding and — "

"Betty," said Jack, "I just want you to know that you've done a superb job so far. And I appreciate it."

"Thanks," she smiled.

"Just continue to be as charming for the rest of the trip, will you?"

"I'll certainly try." Her eyes began to sparkle.

Suddenly he leaned over and kissed her. Betty felt an immediate desire to melt into his arms, but she did not get the opportunity. In the first place, he did not put his arms around her. And secondly, both of them were suddenly aware of Kazuko standing in front of them, grinning and bowing.

"Prease not to interrupt, but would you care for a drink?"

"A splendid idea. What will you have, Betty?" asked Jack.

"A martini, I think," said Betty.

She wasn't thinking. She had never deliberately ordered a martini in her life. They immediately went to one's head. But at that instant her head could not have been in a greater whirl. She could still feel the thrill of Jack's lips on hers. And again, she was aware of that magnetic force about him that seemed to draw her toward him, even against her will. What was it, anyway? What was he doing to her?

"Excellent choice. Make it two," said Jack.

Kazuko disappeared down the winding stair.

"Now why on earth did I order that?" asked Betty with self-reproach.

"Because you're always doing something nutsy," he said, and gave her a wide, engaging smile.

10

BETTY'S first glimpse of Japan was the snow covered cone of Mount Fuji sticking up through a cloud bank. The late afternoon sun gave a pinkish tint to the snow and the clouds. Passengers were informed over the intercom that what they were seeing was a remarkable view of the top of the famous mountain. In a few minutes they would be setting down at Tokyo International Airport. All passengers were directed to their seats and to fasten seat belts.

It had been a long trip but had not seemed like nine hours to Betty. She had been busy getting better acquainted with the members of the group. Most of them were considerably older than she, but there were two men in their thirties who gave her plenty of attention.

George Trumbell represented a marketing concern in San Franciso who handled a number of Japanese imports. He was a friendly, casually dressed fellow who had been to Japan before and offered to help Betty find her way around if she needed it.

"I can assure you I will," she said smiling.

David Nolen was a financial analyst with an investment firm that was looking toward gaining some Japanese capital for investing in the United States. He was neat, wore rather thick glasses, carried a brief case and a small computer. When Betty visited with him during the trip he immediately told her what rate of exchange she could expect when turning dollars into Japanese yen.

They had been served brunch, shown a motion picture, served more cocktails and an afternoon snack before landing. And all the time the little Japanese hostesses were ever present and looking for ways to be helpful.

Jack was being his usual busy self. He had maneuvered Billy out of the window seat and had Betty move over, then he sat beside her for brunch. More and more she was becoming aware of his compelling physical presence. The kiss he had given her in the tea-house-in-the-sky was indelibly etched on her awareness.

The aircraft descended into an atmosphere filled with a grayish smog. Glancing out of the window Betty saw a slate colored bay with indistinct buildings beyond. She saw the runway appear below them. Then the plane glided with hardly a jolt onto the concrete and suddenly they were in Japan. Betty turned her head and grinned at Jack.

"We made it!" she cried happily.

"Was there any doubt?" he asked.

"There was a lot of doubt in my mind. I had no idea I would come until you casually dropped the word in the Press Club back in Honolulu nearly a month ago."

"I'm glad, too, that you're here." He gave her knee a pat.

His touch sent an electric thrill surging through her. Again, his nearness caused her mind to race crazily. She fought to regain her composure, telling herself sternly that she was simply excited over the trip into this land of cherry blossoms and chrysanthemums.

Eagerly, Betty peered through the

aircraft window as the plane taxied up to the ramp, but what she saw was hardly different than she had seen in other airports. Only the workers in coveralls appeared smaller.

"Ladies and gentlemen we have just arrived at our destination. We enjoyed having you aboard our seven-forty-seven garden jet and hope we can serve you again on Japan Air Lines. For those of you who are visiting Japanese Islands for the first time, welcome. We hope you enjoy your stay." Then the voice switched over to the Japanese Language. Betty was pleased to discover that she could follow it well enough to know that the Japanese citizens were being welcomed back home and given the same pitch about using Japan Air Lines the next time they required air transportation.

As the passengers departed, Kazuko gave a special fond *sayonara* to Betty who replied in kind using Japanese. The two girls looked at each other smiling, bridging centuries of time and cultures with their own brief acquaintance. And then it was time for Betty to move along with the others through the unloading compartment and into the Japanese airport terminal building.

Kiyoo Maruyama ushered them all into a large area and had them wait while he cleared their luggage through Customs without inspection. This had been arranged as a courtesy for the trade mission group. Then he led them through the terminal building to a special chartered bus. When the bus took off for the New Otani Hotel, a small Japanese girl in a modern pants suit stood up in the front of the bus and began speaking into a microphone.

"My name is Naoko Tsutomi," she said in English. "And I am to be one of your interpreters while you are in Japan. So you will be seeing a great deal of me. We will get better acquainted later, but right now, for those of you who have never been in Japan before, I will point out a few of the interesting sights as we drive to the hotel which is about thirty minutes away."

Betty was all eyes and ears as the girl pointed out the elevated train, the Tokyo Tower and districts, the names of which meant nothing to Betty. But when the girl announced that they were now in the Akasaka Ku she remembered reading that it was an extremely high rent district containing some of the best restaurants and geisha houses in all of Japan. And the New Otani Hotel was somewhere nearby. The bus arrived there after climbing a hill and making a right turn over a bridge above railways.

As Betty and Jack entered the hotel, he spoke to her quietly.

"You'll want to rest, as we all do. But in about two hours be ready to meet me for cocktails."

"Good grief! After all we had on the plane?" she exclaimed.

"Yes. I'm going to take you to a special place. One that I think you'll enjoy."

"Well, whatever you wish," said Betty shaking her head and wondering if she was up to it.

They were provided with keys to their rooms and told that their luggage would be delivered shortly. In the elevator going up to the eighteenth floor, Betty heard her first authentic Japanese music, a minor key melody fashioned on the oriental scale. She smiled to herself at this touch of the Far East coming over a public electronic system. She found her door and let herself into a comfortable, though somewhat standard, hotel room, but one that seemed to look out over all of Tokyo.

Betty picked up a tourist map of Tokyo and found the location of the New Otani Hotel. But looking out of the window, she had no idea if what she saw was what was listed on the map. She would have to wait to get better oriented.

Right now she needed a relaxing shower. She threw off her clothes and enjoyed a long, restful ten minutes letting the warm water stream against her nakedness. Afterward, she toweled herself vigorously. As she pulled a cover up over her body and stretched out on the comfortable bed, sleep was only a moment away.

The urgent ringing of the phone woke her up.

"I thought I told you to meet me for cocktails!" Jack's impatient voice assaulted her ear.

"Yes. You did, but — "

"Never mind. Are you ready?"

"Well, not quite."

"Get with it. Meet me in the revolving restaurant on the roof in five minutes."

"Jack, I can't possibly. Please give me ten," she begged.

"If I must," he said and hung up.

Betty dressed, fixed her face and brushed her hair faster than she could ever remember. She ran to the elevator. When it came she asked the girl operator for the revolving restaurant. The girl let her off on the top floor into a large area that led to the entrance of the restaurant. There, she looked around for Jack. He was nowhere in sight. She went to the maitre d'hotel's desk and asked if a gentleman had arrived and already taken a table.

"Several gentlemen have. Was there anyone in particular?" asked the Japanese maitre d' with polite cynicism.

"Yes. A Mr. Jack Benning," she said while attempting to wither him with her suddenly narrowed eyes.

He glanced at his reservation list. "I have no one here by that name. But if you care to look around, you are most welcome."

Betty didn't know why the exchange had angered her. She should have been amused, she decided on second thought. She could only guess that she was uptight because Jack was late. Without much hope of finding him, she stepped into the restaurant proper. It was a huge round structure that was revolving almost imperceptibly. The tables were arranged so that the guests could look out at Tokyo as they ate and drank. She walked all around the place but Jack was nowhere to be seen. She wondered what to do next.

"You did not find someone?" the Maitre d' remarked when she came back to his station.

"No. The someone I'm looking for is not here," she said coldly.

"If you care to wait, I will show you to a table."

"Could I wait here?"

"Most assuredly."

Betty waited for twenty minutes, her anger building up with each passing moment. How like Jack to demand that she be here in five minutes, then not show up himself. She began to wonder

208

if she had come to the right place. She decided to call his room and see if something had gone wrong. Just as she began looking for a phone, he sauntered in.

"Now who's late?" she said.

"Sorry. I ran into the fellow from the Trade Center. He told me the material for our exhibits would be delivered at seven o'clock in the morning. I had to get hold of Billy and tell him to be there at that time. And I want you there, too, in order to check off the inventory."

"At seven in the morning?" she groaned.

"We're not here on vacation."

All at once he smiled at her warmly, took her arm and squeezed it. Then he asked the Maitre d' for a table for two. When they were seated she again started to remonstrate, but he disarmed her by leaning forward and peering at her appreciatively.

"You're just as pretty in Tokyo as you were in Honolulu."

"Why is it that every time you make me angry, you follow up by making me glad?" Betty smiled at him helplessly.

Jack laughed and sent a waiter for cocktails. He began pointing out places of interest as the slowly rotating room provided them with a spectacular three hundred and sixty degree panoramic view of the largest city in the world. Slowly the day faded and the lights of Tokyo began twinkling below. Betty was treated to distant neon signs in Japanese calligraphy. She was thrilled at the changing scenery, made even more interesting by Jack's helpful explanations.

All at once, she was happier than she had been in a long, long time.

Later they ordered snacks from the buffet. What came were small helpings of raw fish called *sushi*, fried shrimp *tempura* and bite size beef *sukiyaki*. A colorful little white and blue bottle of sake was placed beside each of their plates. There had been plenty of food during the flight over so neither of them was hungry. But Betty found herself enjoying the snacks. She sat relaxed over her coffee looking out at the Japanese night. Jack fell into a contemplative silence as he too looked out over ancient Tokyo with its modern high rises, millions of people and its Buddha and Shinto shrines. Once again, Betty realized they were enjoying each other's company without feeling the necessity of conversation. That added up to something, she told herself, though she did not know exactly what.

"Getting tired?" Jack asked a while later.

"Sort of."

"So am I."

"Are you still going to make me get up at an ungodly hour in the morning?" She glanced at him, pleading with her eyes.

"Yes. And you'll be working hard all day, believe me. We've an awful lot to get done."

He signed the check and they took the elevator down to her floor. He got off with her and accompanied her to her room.

"Goodnight, Princess Pupule," he said.

Suddenly he took her in his arms and kissed her hard. Her arm came up and went around his neck. When their lips parted, her heart was pounding. She looked up at him, her eyes searching his, questioning, wondering, longing. She felt a long magic moment while they seemed drawn together both in body and spirit. Then all at once, Jack broke the spell.

"See you in the morning." And with that he turned and disappeared around a turn in the corridor without looking back.

Betty let herself into the room. Her knees felt wobbly and there was a sensation in her body as if she were suspended in air. In a daze, though a pleasant one, she managed to get undressed and into her pajamas. She stood by the window for a few minutes trying to sort out her thoughts and emotions. Her attempt met with little success but gradually she relaxed into a wonderful feeling of well being. All the mystery, adventure and romance of the Far East came into focus. How wonderful — !

The phone rang, shattered the thoughts that were drifting through her mind. She hurried to the bedside and picked it up, wondering who would be calling her out here in Japan.

"Just wanted to remind you to leave a call for six in the morning," came Jack's voice.

"Oh, yes, of course — "

"Goodnight."

She started to reply but before any words came he hung up. Betty put down the receiver. Her wide, pretty mouth, widened into a grin that seemed to stretch from ear to ear. He was still thinking about her, just as she was thinking of him. Hey, girl, get hold of yourself, she said. She had almost gotten into bed without remembering to leave a call. She phoned. Thank goodness she hadn't forgotten.

For a few drowsy moments she stared up into the darkness of her room. With everything that had happened during the past few hours, her sleep should have been one of wonderful serenity. But instead she was bothered by strange and disturbing dreams. She was far from rested when the phone rang early the next morning and a soft feminine Japanese voice told her to get up 'prease.'

She could not remember her dreams but she had the distinct impression that they had caused her to feel worn out, now that she was getting up. As she dressed she tried to blame it on the raw fish she had eaten last night. She could not understand it otherwise because her mind was in a state of euphoria thinking back on her evening with Jack. But could it be all that wonderful? She wondered. Maybe she had been wondering in those dreadful dreams.

"Are you up?" came a voice over the phone, when she picked it up in response to its ring.

"Yes." She recognized Billy's voice at the other end.

"Let's have a quick breakfast in the coffee shop, then we'll take a taxi to the Trade Center," he suggested.

"Good. I'll meet you downstairs in just a few minutes."

She and Billy discussed the job ahead over rolls and coffee, a few minutes later. Then they entered a taxi in front of the hotel. He handed the driver written instructions that had been prepared for him by one of the interpreters who were going to be available to the trade mission. The driver looked it over, nodded and took off.

Betty was thrown against Billy, as the taxi whirled around the drive. Then it shot down a narrow winding street on the left side of oncoming traffic. The taxi seemed to have no brakes as it reached the bottom of the hill, crossed over a short bridge and headed for what looked like certain doom as the street dead-headed into a wider avenue.

"My God! Can you tell him to slow down?" cried Billy, imploring her to use her knowledge of Japanese.

"*Motto yukkuri, dozzo!*" 'slow down, please,' she begged the driver.

He looked back at them and grinned and in so doing almost missed the turn. This time Billy was thrown against Betty. The taxi then headed down the Sotobori Dori, a wide street on which was located the United States Trade Center in Tokyo. Five minutes later the taxi screeched to a halt in front of a modern ten story building.

Billy crawled out of the taxi as if he had never expected to set foot on solid ground again. Betty was shaken but otherwise in control of herself. He paid the driver and they entered the building.

"Never again," Billy swore.

"Never again what?" She glanced at him with amusement.

"Never again will I ride in a taxi in Tokyo."

"Forget it. We're here safe and sound," she chided, as they rode in an elevator to the seventh floor.

As they arrived in the room assigned to the trade mission, workmen were bringing in the last of the packages and crates for the exhibit. Betty had brought along a portfolio containing the inventory. Billy took off his coat and they both went to work. At ten o'clock that morning the telephone rang in one corner of the room. Billy answered it.

"Oh, hello, Jack. Yes, Betty's here." He motioned for her to come to the phone. "Jack wants to speak to you."

"Are you about finished with Billy?" he asked when she was on the line.

"We've finished the inventory, if that's what you mean. But now I'm helping him set up the exhibits," she explained.

"Let him finish that part of it. You come back to the hotel. Come to room nine-one-nine. I've got a job for you to do here."

216

"I'll be right there," she replied, and hung up.

That's what she thought. Betty left the Trade Center with her portfolio and waved to a passing taxi that ignored her. Two more came by with passengers in them. Then she failed to spot one for the next ten minutes. She went back into the building and spoke Japanese to a janitor who was cleaning the walls. Where, she asked, could she find a taxi? He failed to understand what she had said and replied in Japanese in such a way that Betty could not understand him. She gave up and went back outside. Again she waved to a taxi. This time, it swung to the curb.

"Do you speak English?" she asked.

The driver gave her a blank look so she tried speaking in Japanese.

"*Otani hoteru, dozzo.*" 'Otani Hotel, please,' she said.

The driver shook his head helplessly.

"*Otani,*" she said again. Then an idea struck her. "*Akasaka Ku.*" she added. Since the New Otani was located in the Akasaka District, she reasoned that this information would help her get her

217

destination across to him.

What Betty did not realize was that they were already in the Akasaka District. The confused driver understood her use of the word Akasaka, but since they were already there he figured she must mean Asakusa District, which was across on the other side of Tokyo.

"*Asakusa*," he said.

It sounded like Akasaka to Betty so she nodded. The driver smiled and they took off. It had taken less than ten minutes to go from the hotel to the Trade Center. But they had already been travelling for twenty minutes and nothing looked like the hotel area to Betty. They were headed along a great wide street lined with impressive buildings, seemingly of a governmental nature. In a sudden panic Betty realized the driver was taking her to the wrong place, whatever he had in mind.

She spoke to him in Japanese. He shook his head.

"*Tomeru nasai!*" she cried, suddenly remembering the word for 'stop'.

The driver jammed on his brakes and pulled over to the curb. They started

218

talking to each other but accomplished nothing. Betty opened the door and got out. She looked around for help. A man who might be an American came by and she called him. He stopped and listened then shook his head. He replied to her in German.

"May I help, Miss?" asked a courteous voice beside her.

Betty turned and saw a young Japanese gentleman smiling at her. She drew a sigh of relief and explained her predicament. He asked her where she wished to go and she told him the New Otani Hotel. The man leaned over and spoke to the driver who grinned and nodded.

"*Domo, arigato gozeimus,*" 'thank you very much,' said Betty gratefully.

The man bowed. "*Doo itashimashite.*" 'It was nothing,' he said.

Betty got back into the taxi and away they went. They arrived at the hotel approximately one hour after Betty had left the Trade Center. Another complication ensued when she dug into her purse and came up with American money. She had neglected to change her dollars into yen. The driver looked dismayed when she showed him what she had to pay with. But again Betty was rescued, this time by a hotel doorman. He paid the taxi driver out of his own pocket, then accompanied Betty inside to a government exchange window. She traded her dollars into yen, reimbursed the door man and thanked him profusely.

"You're most welcome, Miss," he said, in almost perfect English.

Betty hurried to the elevator and went up to the room Jack had indicated. It was a meeting room equipped with tables and several chairs. Two of the men with the trade mission were there with Jack. He did not berate her in front of them, but he looked annoyed.

"Where have you been?" he asked.

"Riding around Tokyo with a taxi driver who could not find the New Otani Hotel," she replied.

"That's my girl," said Jack throwing up his hands. The other men laughed.

Betty was told that she would be working in this room for the next three days, making up packages of materials for the men who were going to start calling on Japanese business men first thing in the morning. She was to keep a ledger of where they went.

The next two days were fairly routine for her. The men came in every morning and set out in pairs or groups of three and four with their interpreters. Most of the interpreters were young men who visited with Betty each morning while waiting to go off on calls. They were fascinated by her blonde hair, never having been exposed to natural blondes, except rarely in other caucasian girls in Japan.

"How do you keep it that way?" one of them asked her one morning.

"I don't do anything. This is the way it is," she replied, smiling.

The young men marveled. One of them said she could make it big on the stage in Japan if she decided not to go home. One of them asked if she had ever been to the Shockiku Revue in the Kokusai theater in Tokyo.

"Never heard of it," said Betty.

"You should go sometime. It's an all-girl review of singers and dancers, some of the best in the Orient. Visitors say it's one of the best attractions in Tokyo," one of the interpreters told her.

Betty made a mental note of it and resolved to go the first chance she had. It came the very next evening, when Jack asked if she would like to get away from the hotel for the evening.

"I'd love it," she replied.

"Any place in particular you'd like to go?" he asked.

"One of the interpreters mentioned a good show in town," said Betty remembering.

"You surely don't want to sit through a Kabuki?"

"That wasn't the name. He said it was an all girl review, and quite good."

"Shockiko in the Kokusai theater?" Jack asked.

"Yes. That's it."

"Ah sooo," he smiled. "Okay I'll take you. I saw it a couple of years ago."

"Then you wouldn't want to see it again. It's not that important to me," she said immediately. She wanted to go somewhere that he would enjoy.

"It's a new show. They change it every

two or three months. Anyway I'd like to see it again."

And so they went, just the two of them late that afternoon. It seemed to Betty that she and Jack were falling into a relationship much closer than she ever could have imagined. He seemed to enjoy her company. And she certainly enjoyed his. It was only his unpredictable behavior that threw her. That, she simply could not understand.

The show was everything it was said to be. Beautifully staged with a dozen different presentations during the course of the show. The singing was quite good, some of the dancing sensational. The chorus line, though not in the class of the Rockettes of Radio City Music Hall, was nonetheless well-trained and gorgeously costumed. Both Betty and Jack enjoyed it immensely.

After the show, they took a taxi to the glittering Ginza district and ate in a small Japanese restaurant. Later, Jack took her for a stroll among the many neon lighted streets, where night clubs, discotheques, restaurants and geisha houses flourished.

"Thanks a million, Jack," she said,

when the evening was over. "I'm having so much fun seeing Japan. Especially with you."

"And I'm having fun showing you around, Princess," he smiled.

And once again, as they parted at the door to her room, he took her in his arms and kissed her. At that moment, she would have gone with him to the ends of the earth if he had asked her. But he didn't. He quickly released her and, without a word, went down the hall to the elevator.

Betty tried to rationalize her feelings toward Jack. But try as she might, she could not make sense out of it. His physical appeal was not to be denied. It was magnetic, compelling, electric. Yet she was at ease in his presence most of the time. It was only during business hours that she felt tense when he was around. But even that she was beginning to control.

She wondered if she was falling in love again. And that caused her to be wary. When the last lingering thought of Lon was gone, she wanted to be sure that the next man would not hurt her. With such an overwhelming person as Jack, being hurt was quite a possibility.

She saw him only briefly the next day and had no idea where he went that following night. When she found out, quite by accident, that he and three other men on the mission had spent the evening in a geisha house, she stiffened with indignation.

That was certainly one way to hurt a girl!

11

"WHAT precisely goes on in a geisha house?" Betty asked Gen Karamatsu the next morning. Gen was one of the interpreters and spoke excellent English.

"Nothing much. For entertainment the girls sing and dance and play musical instruments. Then they sit around and visit with the customers."

"Is that all?" Betty's brown eyes were filed with skepticism.

Suddenly the interpreter realized what she was thinking and laughed.

"That's all. Take my word for it. It's strictly a social evening. Some geisha, of a lesser type, might go in for what you call hanky-panky, but not the good ones."

Betty blushed, but she persisted. "What would the evening be like if some of the men on the trade mission went to a geisha house?"

"As I said. Four of them went last

226

night. One was your boss, but I guess you already knew that. I know where they went. It was one of the most expensive and prestigious in Tokyo. Only wealthy business men, diplomats and important visitors go there. It was an honor for them to be invited."

"They were invited?" Betty was surprised.

"Yes. Some Japanese business men wished to show them our hospitality."

"Are girls ever invited to geisha houses?" she asked, just out of curiosity.

"Rarely. But if you wish it can be arranged."

"Oh no! I didn't mean that. I'm not interested, just wondering."

"I think you would find it quite boring," he explained. "There is nothing else in the world quite like a Japanese geisha. Only Japanese men can appreciate her. Japan, don't forget, is still a man's country. The wives mostly stay home, even though they appear to be liberated these days."

Betty gave up trying to figure it all out. She waited for Jack to tell her he had gone to a geisha house, but he said nothing about it. It was his silence on the subject, she finally concluded, that had thrown her nose out of joint. She ended up telling herself that it was none of her business and that she didn't care where he went or what he did. She was right in the first instance but not the second. She was beginning to care. She was not falling in love with him, she maintained staunchly. But she did care a little, she had to admit to herself.

The following evening the trade mission group gave a cocktail party and reception for the Japanese business men they had called upon. It was held at the Tokyo America Club near the Tokyo tower. Jack warned Betty to be ready to go with him on time, and by all means to dress up for the occasion. She had brought a long dress with her for the occasion and hoped she could make him proud.

And she did. Everyone at the party was attentive to her. And she was extremely flattered when the honored guest, the American Ambassador to Japan and his wife, spent several moments chatting with her and showing interest in her impression of Tokyo. The Japanese business men, to whom she was introduced, were intrigued with her blonde good looks just as other Japanese had been.

Jack, she noticed, looked at her approvingly as she circulated among the guests. He was as busy as a politician running for office. He was determined to exchange greetings with each guest there and succeeded, though he was moving about from the moment the first guests arrived until the room was empty and the bar closed.

"I think we pulled it off well," he told her and Billy as the three of them rode back to the hotel in a taxi late that evening. "Let's go up to the roof bar for a nightcap."

"I had enough at the cocktail party," said Billy plaintively. He had complained daily of being worn out. He had never gotten over the jet lag and on top of all that he had been working like a dog. "I'm going to bed, if you don't mind. And I'm also going to cancel out on the sightseeing trip tomorrow."

When Betty and Jack were alone, he said, "I'm glad Billy decided to turn in.

It will be much more relaxing, just the two of us."

Once again Betty looked at him and her eyes softened. A magic spell little by little was coming over her every time she was alone with Jack. Something irresistible seemed to be happening between them. At least, she felt it. She wondered if he felt it too?

They sat at the roof-top bar, seventeen stories above the darkened labyrinths of sprawling Tokyo. This time they were not on the revolving part. They drank a toast to the success of the party and to the rest of the trip. Tomorrow, neither had to work. A tour for the group had been arranged and the bus would be leaving early the next morning for Yokohama, Kamakura, Hakone, Owakadani and other points of interest.

"I'm looking forward to tomorrow," said Jack. "I've never been to Hakone but I've heard it's beautiful. It's on a lake up in the mountains, you know."

Betty did not know it. She had had very little time to study the itinerary for tomorrow. In fact, she had given little thought to this part of the trip. It was enough that she was getting to see Tokyo and Osaka while in Japan. But she, too, looked forward to going, mainly because she would be with Jack.

But the next morning when the bus was loaded and nearly ready to depart, Jack was nowhere to be seen. Betty asked George Trumbull if he knew where Jack was.

"Nope. But I guess he'll be along at the last minute, as usual."

"We're ready to go," said Naoko Tsutomi, the same girl who had been on the bus in from the airport. "Is Mr. Benning coming?"

"Yes. I can't imagine what's holding him up," said Betty.

"If we're to make our schedule today we should leave in the next five minutes," said the Japanese girl. "Why don't you call his room."

Betty hurried into the hotel to a house phone. She was surprised when Jack answered immediately.

"Jack," she cried. "We're all waiting for you. Is anything wrong?"

"I can't go. Tell the party I'm sorry."

"Are you sick?" she asked anxiously.

"No."

"Then — ?"

"Look. All of you go on. I've got to wait for a long distance call from Hawaii."

"Oh dear, something has gone wrong at the office?" she asked, wondering whether Audrey or Warson had called.

"No. It's not from the office." He hesitated, then added. "Cheryl is trying to reach me and I've got to be here when she calls."

"I see." Betty's voice suddenly went flat.

"Tell the folks I'm sorry that I can't go. All of you have a good time."

"Sure," said Betty and hung up.

The day should have been one of great enjoyment for Betty. She had looked forward eagerly to this sightseeing trip. But now a pall had fallen over the whole thing. It seemed impossible that the girl back in Hawaii could exert her influence on Jack this far away. Yet, she had thrown him off-schedule with his clients and had landed a low blow on Betty. She wondered why Jack had not taken a firm stand and told Cheryl her

232

call would have to wait until he returned this evening.

Everyone but Betty was in an expectant mood as the bus left from in front of the New Otani. She stared glumly out the window as they headed south through Yokohama and through miles of crowded streets, stores and small homes that were covered by indestructible green tile roofs. After a while the urban sprawl gave way to rice paddies and small communities with occasional factories located around a cluster of apartments. Her mind was back at the hotel with Jack when the road began skirting a foggy sea and mountains were rising on the other side of the four lane highway. All at once she gave a start as someone tapped her on the shoulder.

"You're mighty quiet, Miss Lane."

She looked around. It was Fred Leyhe who was sitting with his wife in the seat directly behind hers. Betty managed a smile.

"I guess I'm just relaxing. I've been terribly busy for the past few days."

"And you've done a good job, too. We all appreciate it," Fred replied. He went on to comment that she was the only representative of Benning & Associates on the bus.

"Golly. I hadn't realized it, but it's true," she said, sitting up. No matter what Jack was up to with Cheryl, or vice versa, she had an obligation to be a good representative of the agency.

From then on, she forced herself to leave her seat and move along the aisle of the bus, making small talk with members of the group.

Naoko Tsutomi, the Japanese girl guide, occasionally addressed the group by means of the microphone in the front of the bus, pointing out places of interest. Toward the middle of the morning she announced that they were approaching Kamakura, their first stop, where they would visit the world famous great bronze Buddha. A short time later the bus threaded through a small two lane road and backed into a cramped parking area surrounded by high banks of conifers and vines. The air was heavy with moisture as they left the bus and followed Naoko up a winding path and steps into the park-like area that surrounded the towering Buddha.

"I've seen pictures of that ever since I was a little girl," Betty exclaimed, staring up at the bronze casting.

"Do you know I have too and I didn't really realize what we were coming to see until just now." It was George Trumbull, standing beside Betty.

She looked around at him and smiled. He took out his camera and had Betty stand between him and the statue. After he had clicked the shutter he said,

"You'll be a lot prettier in the picture than that thing in back of you."

"Don't talk that way," she laughed. "The Buddha might not like it and put the whammy on you."

George accompanied her back to the bus when Naoko announced it was time. The bus took them on from there to Hakone, one of the most celebrated resorts in Japan, in time for lunch.

"Let's have a cocktail," George suggested as he and Betty sat down at a table together.

"Thank you. Don't mind if I do," she replied.

She didn't know why, but she thought George's suggestion was just great. All morning she had felt a smoldering resentment, just below the surface, at Cheryl Canton. A drink might put a different focus on things. But it achieved just the opposite. In spite of George's pleasant conversation during lunch, Betty felt worse than ever. She was glad when they left the restaurant and boarded a huge catamaran motor vessel that took them across beautiful Lake Ashi nestled in the mountains.

On the other side of the lake they were taken to Owakadani where the odor of sulfur from the hot springs combined with the drink to cause Betty extreme discomfort. For a few frantic minutes she thought she was going to be sick.

But the cool air when they arrived at the Fujiya Hotel helped to revive her. This was the last stop before they went to Odawara and caught the late afternoon bullet train back to Tokyo. It was nearly eight o'clock at night before they got back to the New Otani. The first thing Betty did when she was in her room was to call Jack.

"I just wanted to report that we're all back safe and sound," she told him, hoping he would brief her on his call from Cheryl.

"That's good. I suppose everyone enjoyed the trip."

"It would have been better if you had been along."

"Really." His voice sounded distant and aloof.

"Jack. Is anything wrong?" she asked finally.

"Oh, no."

"Then why — You don't sound right."

"How should I sound?"

"I don't know, but I wish you would be honest with me. What is it?"

He hesitated before saying anything. "I wonder which one of us needs to be honest."

"Now just what is that supposed to mean?"

"You never did tell me about yourself, Betty. That's what it means."

"I don't get it!"

"Okay, maybe it will help if I tell you that you've been on the rebound ever since leaving St. Louis. I don't like to be taken for a handy man to have around."

237

"Whatever on earth are you talking about?" Betty demanded.

"I learned this morning that you've been in love with a fellow back in St. Louis all along. And I understand he's a married man at that!" he said evenly.

Betty was stunned. She could hardly believe her ears. How in the world had Jack found out about Lon Holderness? She recovered herself and spoke in a voice that had suddenly gone hoarse.

"Is that why Cheryl called you this morning? She wanted to tell you that?"

"No, she called about some other matters, but mentioned it before she hung up."

Betty bet she did! For the first time in her life she felt actual rage. She knew why Cheryl had called Jack. Through the turmoil inside her head she heard Jack's expressionless voice.

"I've got to go now. See you in the morning."

And then the receiver went dead in her hand.

Betty slept very little that night. She could not get it out of her mind that Cheryl Canton had managed, somehow, to find out about her and Lon and had thrown it at her halfway around the globe. The only person she had mentioned it to since moving to Hawaii was Audrey Ching. Could Audrey have deliberately or accidentally mentioned it to Cheryl? Betty simply did not know what to think.

But her concern at the moment was more important. It was the effect the information had on Jack. His voice had seemed most expressive to her over the phone, not by what he said so much as the way he had said it. His faith in her had been shaken. That had come through. And yet, she knew she had to see him in person to sense how he really felt. Then she would have to assure him, somehow, that the affair was long since over and that Lon Holderness meant nothing to her. She lay awake most of the night, or so it seemed; thinking, wondering and trying to decide what to do.

Once during the night, she grew so restless that she arose and paced around the darkened hotel room. She told herself that she was being melodramatic and that she had to get some sleep. The self-admonition did not help. She went to the window and looked out at the night stars over Tokyo, at Orion and Betleguese and Ursa Minor. She besought the mysticism of the Far East for some answers but none came. That contemplative Buddha that she had seen just that day at Kamakura, what did it know of the troubles that beset her? Nothing, she decided. Things were no different in the Orient than they were back home. Somehow she had to work out her own destiny. She wondered if there ever would come a time in her life when things would be right and trouble free? Or was she one of those persons who was trouble prone?

An eastern light was driving darkness from the sky when Betty finally lay down on the bed and dozed. Abruptly, she awoke to discover that it was broad daylight. Quickly she glanced at her watch. It was only seven-thirty but further sleep was impossible. She got up and stood under the shower, letting the water splatter down her shoulders and back providing her with a hydro-massage. It helped a little, at any rate, to relieve her tension. As she dried herself her stomach let her know that there had been nothing in it since yesterday noon at Hakon. Her call to Jack last night had so upset her that she had forgotten all about having dinner.

She dressed slowly, deliberately, as if she had to start this day with the greatest of care and caution. At eight o'clock she went down to the coffee shop. She had no appetite, even though her stomach growled, but she ate because she knew she should. A half a grapefruit, sweet roll and coffee sufficed.

"I've been looking for you," said Jack, coming into the coffee shop just as she was finishing. His eyes met hers only briefly. "We've got a job to do. Billy is sick. I've been up to his room and he's got a fever. He'll have to stay in bed."

"Oh, I'm sorry." Betty instantly put her own concern aside. "Do you know what it is that's wrong?"

"It might be the flu or some other bug out here. You never really know what you might pick up in Asia."

"Can I take anything up to him?" she asked.

"No. At the moment the best thing for him is to stay in bed and sleep. It's the exhibit that needs attention. He was supposed to take it down today but he's in no condition for that. You and I will have to go to the Trade Center and see what our next move should be."

"I'm ready right now," she said quickly, hoping that her willingness would penetrate the shield that he seemed to have put up between them.

"First I have to see about the arrangements to get us all the way to Osaka at noon." He glanced at his wristwatch. "It's eight-thirty now. Meet me in the lobby at a quarter after nine."

Before she could say anything further to him, he left the coffee shop. Betty was thankful that he needed her for something. Only time would tell if she could talk to him about the information he had received from Cheryl. She took one more sip of coffee, then went to her room and hurriedly gave herself an inspection. She wanted to look her best for Jack. It was the only thing she knew to do at the moment. Then she hurried to the lobby and waited.

"Let's go," he said hurrying up to her a few minutes later.

They took a taxi to the Trade Center. Jack found the building manager, who spoke very little English, and brought him to the exhibition room. Between Jack and Betty speaking Japanese they finally got through to him that they wanted all the material packaged and sent to the Benning & Associates Public Relations Agency in Hawaii.

"*Hi, wakarimasu,*" 'I understand,' he said bowing low to each of them.

It was agreed that he would take care of everything, so it turned out to be less of a job than Betty had figured. Lucky that they had not planned to use much of the material in Osaka. What little was needed, she and Jack managed to fit into a large box which they took back to the hotel with them.

"Now I've got another job for you."

"I'll do anything you say," Betty replied fervently. "Anything!"

"You're going to have to take charge of seeing that the group gets from here into the Royal Hotel in Osaka."

"But — ?"

243

"It's all arranged. You know the schedule as well as I do. Naoka Tsutomi will be on hand to help. I'm not going."

"Not going?" Betty stared at him. "Why?"

"I've got to see that Billy is taken care of. I might have to put him in a hospital, or send him back home if he's up to it."

She could not help admiring his loyalty to his employee and she wondered if he'd do the same for her under similar circumstances. She guessed that he would. After all, she was nothing more than an employee.

"Will you join us in Osaka later?"

"I'll fly down either tonight or tomorrow, depending on Billy's condition."

At least she was relieved to know that. The way he had started out, she wondered if he had suddenly decided to abandon the group. But that would not be like him. She tried to meet his eyes with hers, but he avoided looking toward her. Instead, he told her she had better do her last minute packing and get back to the lobby to meet with the other members of the trade mission.

Half an hour later, Betty was back, as he had requested. Her luggage was packed and ready to be picked up outside her room. A few members of the party had already arrived. She wondered if she would see Jack before they left, or whether he would leave it up to her to cope with arrangements as best she could. But he appeared only ten minutes before the bus was to take them to the railway station where they would board the bullet train for Osaka.

"Folks," he said, raising his voice so all could hear. "I have an announcement. I will be unable to leave with you for Osaka. Billy Everett is ill. I think it's the flu but we don't know yet. Anyway, I want to see what I can do for him, possibly getting him on a plane back to Hawaii, if the doctor says I should. I hope to catch up with you in Osaka and be ready to start making calls with you either tomorrow or the next day, as originally planned. Meanwhile. Miss Lane will be the one to contact, if you need any assistance from Benning & Associates."

"Miss Lane will do fine," George Trumbull spoke up and with that Betty was given a round of applause.

"Naoka is really the one who is in charge of getting us to Osaka," said Betty. "And now I think the bus is waiting outside to take us to the station."

She tried to get Jack alone to tell him goodbye and good luck with Billy but others were talking with him. She glanced over her shoulder as they moved outside. Jack had turned away and was walking toward the elevators. With a heavy heart, Betty followed the others onto the bus.

12

BETTY preferred to be alone with her thoughts as the sleek super-express train raced toward Osaka at 125-miles per hour. She sat staring unseeing through a large window but her isolation was short lived. Members of the group kept stopping by her seat, asking about Billy and visiting with her about many other things. She did her best to sound interested and congenial, but with Jack's attitude worrying her, putting up a good front was not easy.

An hour or so out of Tokyo, Naoko told her that there was a dining car two cars back where she could get some time to herself. She went back to the car which was fitted with a lunch counter on one side and a service and sandwich bar on the other. She bought a sandwich and coffee from one of the clerks and found an empty seat at the lunch counter. For a while she enjoyed the luxury of her own solitude, looking out at the passing rice paddies and the mountains in the distance.

When three men from the group showed up she talked with them for a few minutes, then finished her sandwich and returned to her seat.

She could still feel the icy disregard that Jack had shown toward her after hearing from Cheryl Canton. He was much more sensitive than she had ever suspected. She found herself giving into self-pity and despair. Was she doomed to be star-crossed with every man she met? Grimly she took hold of herself. Bob and Marie Walker were sitting two seats back. To get her mind off of herself she arose and went back, spending the rest of the trip visiting them and other members of the mission.

Early that afternoon they arrived in Osaka, that thriving industrial city on the Inland Sea. Naoko led them to another chartered bus which delivered them to the Royal Osaka Hotel some twenty minutes ride from the railway station.

Betty waited with the Japanese girl in the lobby until she was sure everyone in the party had their room keys and that their luggage was being delivered. She was about to go to her room when Naoko asked her to stay a few minutes.

"You look tired, Miss Lane. Anything wrong?"

"No. I guess I'm just tired, as you said."

"You're not getting the flu, I hope. Like Billy."

"I hope not too." Betty smiled wanly.

"Come with me. It will do you good to relax yourself before you go to your room."

Betty had no desire to spend any more time in the lobby. All she wanted was to get up to her own room, under a shower and then to bed for a nap. But Naoko was so polite and showed such concern that she did not want to offend her by turning her down. The Japanese girl took her to a part of the hotel that resembled a garden around a small, beautifully landscaped lake. Beyond was a large waterfall. Kimonoed hostesses waited on the customers who sat in deep comfortable chairs at small marble topped tables.

"Have some coffee or tea and a pastry. They're delicious here," said Naoko.

Betty ordered coffee and the tour guide took tea. After the waitress had brought the beverages she went off but returned immediately with a large tray of French pastry for them to choose from.

"Everything looks good. What would you recommend, Naoko?" Betty asked.

"You like chocolate? I do." And she pointed to a dark, delicious looking devil's food cake.

Betty ordered the same.

"I was sorry Mr. Benning could not be with us yesterday," said Naoko. "I hope nothing is wrong with him."

"No. Nothing is wrong. Just business."

"He is a very tense young man," the Japanese girl observed.

Betty agreed.

"Is he that way all the time?"

"No. Not always."

"You are his secretary, yes?"

"Correct." Betty suddenly sensed that the girl was leading to something. She glanced at her closely.

"Massage his shoulders once in a while as he sits at his desk. That can work wonders with a man."

Betty stared at the girl, thinking she was kidding. But Naoko was deadly serious. She finished eating her pastry and daintily put a napkin to her lips.

"You will do that, yes?"

"I don't know. I've never tried it. It isn't done that I know of in America."

Naoko thought for a moment before she replied. "It would do you good too, to make him relaxed."

"I'm okay," said Betty somewhat defensively.

"Forgive me for saying so, but you like Mr. Benning very much. I have noticed how you look at him."

Good grief, thought Betty, was it that bad? Was she wearing her heart on her sleeve, as she once had with Lon? Her life was getting more and more complicated, but here in Osaka a Japanese girl whom she hardly knew was, in fact, telling her that she was as easily read as a book.

"You're very observant," said Betty.

"Japanese women sometimes look for such things. It's one way of knowing what's going on. I like you. Everyones does. I hope your boss does too." She smiled and stood up.

"Thanks, Naoko."

They parted and Betty went to her room. Her luggage had already been delivered. She took out a pants suit and a dress and hung them in a closet so they would free themselves of wrinkles. After a shower she lay down on the bed, hoping for a nap. It soon became out of the question for her mind turned to the startling suggestion Naoko had made. Betty did not see how she could do such an unconventional thing. It was silly to even think of it. And yet Naoko's words had sounded plausible as she uttered them. Imagine — massaging Jack's shoulders as he sat at his desk. What a presumption that would be on her part! And what a surprise to him!

The first thing on the schedule the following morning was a briefing session for the trade mission members. It was to be a breakfast in a private dining room. Betty arrived early with her notes, her secretarial book and pencils. They were all to be welcomed by the president of the Osaka Chamber of Commerce. Jack was nowhere in sight as the breakfasts were served. He was supposed to introduce the speaker, but he may not have gotten away from Tokyo. Betty got George Trumbull aside.

"Jack doesn't seem to be here yet. Maybe he didn't get in last night. Would you mind introducing the speaker? Here's a paragraph about him. All you have to do is read it," she explained.

"Why don't you do it?" asked George.

"I can't do a thing like that," she said as if the suggestion was preposterous.

"Why not? You make a far better impression than any of us men do." He grinned.

"No way — besides, you know good and well our Japanese speaker would be insulted if I introduced him."

"I wouldn't be if you introduced me."

"Please be serious."

At that instant Jack hurried in. He spotted Betty and came over to her. She explained that she had been trying to get George to introduce the speaker but now that he was here — no problem.

"I'm glad you have no problems," he said cryptically.

"How's Billy?"

"He's one of the problems. He's pretty sick. I'm to call later this afternoon. If he isn't any better we might have to put him in a hospital. He may be coming down with pneumonia."

"Good heavens!" she exclaimed, appalled.

Jack took charge of the meeting after all had finished breakfast. It was routine with him. He introduced the speaker and they all listened for fifteen minutes to a speech welcoming them to Osaka. The business men of Osaka were looking forward to the visits from the personnel of the trade mission. It was the usual expression of good will and welcome.

Betty went to her room after the meeting broke up and worked until nearly noon, bringing her journal up to date and checking some accounts that Jack had given her to keep track of. It helped keep her mind off of Billy, sick and alone in Tokyo. At noon when she went downstairs to the coffee shop for a sandwich, she could not help feeling as if she should be doing something for him; although she had no idea what. She worried about him, as a fellow worker and a good friend.

She finished her lunch at one o'clock. Reviewing the afternoon ahead, she knew the men would not be back from their calls until late that afternoon. There was nothing she could do for them and nothing she could do for Billy. So she decided to do a little sightseeing on her own.

Osaka, she discovered, was not scenic. The central point of interest was the Osaka Castle, which she glimpsed at a distance. However, the city had modern department stores and a myriad of small shops so she spent most of the afternoon just browsing through the colorful streets so narrow that no car could have possibly gotten through. Except for the Palace grounds and the Government buildings, Osaka was much like Tokyo though smaller. It was wall-to-wall people, in any event.

She returned to the hotel around five o'clock and called Jack's room. No answer. She left a message for him to phone her as soon as he could. She was anxious about Billy. And she also hoped that Jack and she might have dinner together. She needed an opportunity to break down the barrier he had set up between them; and to assure him that she had no lingering interests in Lon. But no call came.

Bleakly, she went up to a French restaurant atop the hotel, sat at a table by herself and ordered dinner. She was not interested in the food when it arrived, but she forced herself to eat. She had to keep up her strength. Having been exposed to Billy, when he was coming down with the flu, made her and everyone else vulnerable. All she needed was to get sick in Japan. That would fix everything good, she thought bitterly. Jack would never forgive her. After dinner, for lack of anything else to do, she went to the lobby. She had been there for a few minutes when she ran into the Leyhes.

"Have either of you seen Jack?" she asked.

"Not since around four o'clock," said Fred.

"Is that when you got back from the calls?"

"Yes."

"Thanks." He had ample opportunity to contact her and let her know about Billy. Why hadn't he?

"If we see him we'll tell him you're looking for him."

"Oh, please don't bother. It's not that important." If he didn't think it was, why should she?

And yet, she did. She went to the desk and inquired if there were any messages for her. There were none. Jack was deliberately avoiding her. That was coming through loud and clear. But he might, at least, have let her know about Billy. She *was* concerned about *him*. She went to her room and, for lack of anything else better to do, turned on the television set.

A modern Japanese motion picture with excellent color photography was showing. Betty listened to the dialogue and made out some of the conversation but she found it difficult to follow the story. Soon she was tired of it and turned it off.

She called Jack's room again. Still no answer. It was getting late and she began to worry. Maybe something had happened to him. All sorts of dire consequences raced through her mind. Accidents. Robbery. Assault. But only the accident idea made any sense. Robbery and assault were practically unknown in Japan. It was beneath the Japanese character to lose face by engaging in such uncouth behavior.

Finally, she went to bed. But once again sleep would not come. Betty was beginning to despair of ever getting rested. She stared up into the darkness, worrying and wondering about Jack and — finally admitting to herself — longing for him. Finally a merciful drowziness came over her. She drifted into an undisturbed slumber.

When the telephone awakened her, it was broad daylight. She picked up the receiver. It was Jack.

"You left a note for me to call you," he said.

"That was yesterday."

"What did you want?"

"You said you were going to make a call to find out Billy's condition."

"That's right, and I did."

"Well, how is he?" Suddenly her voice

was edged with anger.

"His fever broke and his temperature is back to normal. He needs to regain his strength; then he'll be all right."

"All this time you left me to worry," she accused.

"Sorry about that," he said casually, "but George and Frank Baker had rented a car and wanted me to drive up to Kyoto with them for dinner. We didn't get back until quite late."

"You might have called."

"At three in the morning. Are you kidding?"

"Yes, even at three in the morning, damn it!" she shot back.

"Hey, what's eating you?"

"Being treated as if I didn't exist." Her anger had gotten the upper hand. It overcame her better judgment.

"Oh, you exist all right. A person only has to be around you awhile to find that out. Now quit pouting and meet me in the coffee shop in fifteen minutes."

Once again Betty was left holding a dead receiver. She slammed it down into its cradle. Her eyes were afire. Who did Jack think he was? Did he always treat people like this? She had just about had her fill of his cavalier ways. Nevertheless, she hurried into her clothes and, fifteen minutes later, appeared in the coffee shop. For a change she did not have to wait for Jack. He was sitting with George and Frank having breakfast.

"You should have been with us last night," said George, when she joined them.

"I wasn't invited," she snapped and shot a glance at Jack. He was buttering an English muffin and did not even notice.

"We went to Kyoto," George informed her.

"So I've been told."

"Did you hear where we went in Kyoto?"

The men smiled at each other significantly. All except Jack. He was giving his attention to his breakfast.

"No."

"A restaurant-night club. And was it something!"

Betty was not interested in George's account of their evening. So it was plenty of booze, food and dancing girls. So what? That sort of thing goes on all over the world. She wanted to know why Jack had left without saying a word to her. It was not until after breakfast that she was alone with him.

"Do you really think it was fair to go off without letting me know about Billy?" she demanded.

"I told you I was sorry," he replied.

"And then you take off leaving me to worry without knowing where you are and — "

"Just one cotton picking minute! Since when do I have to account to you for where I go and what I do?" His voice had an edge to it and his face darkened.

"You don't but — "

"All right then. Just remember that!" It was a command.

Betty knew at once that she had gone too far. She was behaving like a fishwife. After all, Jack was not beholden to her. He was her boss. *She* was beholden to *him*. For some time she had been thinking of their relationship entirely in the wrong light. It was time she faced reality, got back down to earth. Thankfully, this was their last day in

Osaka. Tomorrow they would go back to Tokyo and catch an overnight flight to Honolulu.

To overcome her feeling of dejection, Betty plunged into her work. A farewell party for the trade mission was being held tonight in a Japanese restaurant, but one that specialized in western food. She said no more to Jack and did not see him again until late that afternoon. She was in the lobby mailing postcards to Peg Waters and Mr. Placer, when Jack entered the hotel.

"Be ready to go to the dinner at seven o'clock. I'll meet you in the lobby," he said.

"Yes, sir," said Betty, emphasizing the 'sir'.

He shot her an exasperated look, then went to the elevator. Betty bought some Japanese toothpaste and some perfume in one of the many stores in the lower arcade, then went to her room to get ready.

She was in the lobby at the appointed time and startlingly pretty in a one piece blue cotton knit that revealed her exciting curves.

A chartered bus waited outside the hotel to take the group to the restaurant that was across town. Betty was visiting with other members of the mission when Jack came out of the elevator. She saw his eyes take note of her appearance and thought she saw approval reflected in them.

Half an hour later they arrived at a modern building. The restaurant was on the top floor and looked out at Osaka glittering in the early evening. A full moon was coming up over the mountains toward the east.

Everyone was in a festive mood during the cocktail hour before dinner. Everyone but Betty. She kept up a good pretense as she visited and chatted with the many friends she had made on the trip. In time, though, she knew they would all go their separate ways. Some she would forget and others remember. A few might remain good friends for life. She would be forever grateful to Jack for bringing her along, even though it was ending with their relationship strained.

Betty resolved to go back to being a good secretary. There was no use aspiring to anything more. Whatever her fate might be with Jack or any other man was something that would just happen. She would not try to control it. That was the easiest way out. It was not the most satisfactory way and it was against her natural inclination, but she had tried too hard with Jack and had alienated him by doing so.

After dinner a microphone and podium was set up and Jack provided the group with a quick run-down of their accomplishments in Japan. He recited figures that Betty had compiled as to how many calls they had made on Japanese business men and he read a summary of how effective their work had been. It would be months before any real results would be known, when and if trade agreements would be forthcoming and money would start looking for places to invest.

When he finished, Fred Leyhe went to the microphone.

"Some of us got to thinking a few days ago that we would like to present mementos to the two people who have been most responsible for our success.

264

First, would you come up here, Jack?"
Fred motioned for Jack to return to the
podium, which he did, looking completely
surprised.

"This is for you on behalf of the
trade mission group." Fred handed Jack
a small package wrapped in white paper
and tied with a red ribbon. "It's a token
of our appreciation for all you have
done."

"Thanks, Fred. And to all of you,
thank you very much," said Jack.

It was the first time Betty had ever seen
Jack caught flat-footed. He obviously had
not expected anything like this to happen.
But he was pleased as he returned to his
chair beside Betty.

"And now the other member of the
team. Betty will you come up?" asked
Fred.

Her jaw dropped. There was applause
as she stood up and made her way to the
podium. Why on earth did they want to
honor her? All she had done was her job
and, maybe not even that too well.

Fred smiled. He looked at the other
members of the group. "Four of the men
including myself took it upon ourselves

to buy Jack's gift. But we asked the wives among us to do some shopping for Betty." With that he picked up another box, somewhat larger than the one he had handed Jack, that was wrapped in red paper and tied with a blue ribbon.

"On behalf of all of us, Betty, please accept this present as a token of our appreciation. You were not only Jack's girl Friday, but you were girl Friday and general trouble shooter for all of us."

"Thanks," she stammered and felt her cheeks grow warm. "I — I'll never forget you all, and never forget this trip. Thank you all for the gift. And I must say thanks again to my boss for bringing me along."

"If we ever go again, we'll insist that Jack bring you along next time too," Fred concluded with a laugh.

Applause broke out again as Betty returned to her chair. That concluded the program, such as it was. Fred announced that the bus would be waiting at the entrance to the building to take them all back to the Osaka Royal Hotel.

"And don't forget. We are all to be in the lobby at noon tomorrow, ready to head for the airport," he called as the group made ready to leave the restaurant.

Jack told Betty goodnight in the lobby of the hotel, then turned to the others as they headed for the elevators. He added one more thing to Betty — that he had some papers and receipts that he would give her in the morning to put into the portfolio. Betty went to her room.

The first thing she did was open the gift package. It was a garment of some sort. She took it out of the box. It was, of all things, a hoppi coat. To be sure it was an expensive one made of red silk and with calligraphy brocaded in white and gold. But still it was a hoppi coat.

Now she knew two people who owned hoppi coats. Herself and Cheryl Canton's gardener, she thought caustically. She tossed the coat over the back of the straight chair at the dressing table. Then she took off her clothes and went to bed.

At eight o'clock the next morning Betty stood before her suitcase in nothing but a pair of panty briefs and high heels, finishing her packing. The pants suit that she would wear on the plane was hanging in the closet. At that moment an unexpected knock came at the door of her hotel room.

She looked around for something to put on and noticed the hoppi coat still draped over the chair where she had left it last night. She grabbed it, put it on and tied the belt around her slim waist. She went to the dor.

"Yes?" she inquired as she opened it. To her astonishment Jack was standing there, a set of papers in his hand.

He looked at her. His eyes went up and down her, from her high heels and trim hips to the hoppi coat. Then his eyes met hers.

"Where," he asked, still staring at her, "did you get that?"

"This is what they gave me in the gift box last night."

"It's beautiful."

"Do you want to come in?" she asked.

She turned back into the room. Jack followed her. She noticed in the mirror that he was still admiring her.

"What did they give you?" she asked. "If it's any of my business."

"A travel case. I certainly didn't need one, but I've never had one this nice. The main thing to me was the thought behind it."

"Exactly as I feel about mine."

"Have you figured out what the Japanese characters mean?"

Betty gave a mirthless smile. "Probably Watanabe's Osaka Fish Market Bowling Team. I've had a thing against hoppi coats ever since I did some shopping for one back at the Ala Moana. Remember?"

"I remember something," said Jack, genuinely puzzled.

"Well don't worry about it. What can I do for you?" Somehow Betty felt completely relaxed and in control of herself.

Jack dragged his eyes away from her trim figure and handed her the papers he held. "They're receipts and other documents that I've picked up on the trip. Mainly receipts for taxis and meals. I'll need all this for a final report and also for Internal Revenue Service at tax time. Please keep them in the portfolio."

"Okay." She took them and stuffed them into the large envelope.

"Have you had breakfast?" he said.

"No."

"Then I'll order us up something," he said and went to the phone and called room service.

"I still have some packing to do and then I'll have to change," Betty pointed out.

"Don't let me stop you. What would you like for breakfast?"

Betty had him order a glass of tomato juice, toast and coffee for her. He ordered the same for himself, then sat down in an easy chair by the window.

She finished packing, conscious that his eyes were on her. She wondered if she should carry her pants suit into the bathroom and finish dressing in there. But just then the man arrived with their breakfasts. He set it up for them on a small table and dragged chairs to the opposite sides.

"Now, tell us something," said Jack, before he left. "What do these characters on the young lady's hoppi coat mean?"

The Japanese waiter grinned and replied in good English. "That means 'love'."

270

"Is that all?" asked Jack.

"Yes, but in Japanese that tells it all." He bowed to both of them, then left pulling the door shut behind him.

Jack studied her a moment as she stood by the table ready to sit down. She waited, aware that her appearance had caught his attention from the moment she had let him into the room. She did not know what was all that great about it, but she was highly pleased over the result.

For once she had disturbed Jack without wrecking his car, being late for work, making faces at his girl friend or any other silly or superficial reason. She had disturbed him with her own physical attraction. No girl could fail to get satisfaction from that.

Betty enjoyed her breakfast better than any she'd had since her arrival in the Pacific.

13

"WELCOME Home."
The first thing that greeted Betty, when she entered the apartment at ten o'clock the morning of her arrival back in Honolulu, was a large hand-printed sign that Audrey had made and pinned to Betty's pillow.

It was thoughtful of the Chinese girl, Betty admitted, but it was no amends for betraying her confidences to Cheryl Canton. At the first opportunity she wanted to find out just how Cheryl had learned about Lon.

The trip home had been uneventful. The group had shrunk to half as many as had set out on the junket. The others had elected to spend more time in the Orient; some going to Hong Kong, Singapore and Bangkok. One couple had arranged to go around the world.

Betty was tired. She discovered that jet lag is worse going from west to east then the other way around. She had slept a few hours on the plane. Jack, in the seat behind her, had gotten at least six hours rest. They cleared customs at Honolulu International Airport and the two of them took a taxi, with Jack dropping her off at her apartment and then going to his own.

"You needn't show up at the office today," he had said. "You'll need the day to get rested."

"Thanks, but I can come in after lunch. I think I'll be rested enough by then," she replied.

"That's what you think. I've made this trip before. You'll still be tired this time tomorrow. Take the day off. That's what I'm going to do, after I call the office."

"If you insist. And, Jack — "

"Yes?"

"Again thanks a million."

"For what?"

"For taking me to Japan."

He smiled and shrugged, but there was no departing kiss. He was still morose over learning about her broken romance in St. Louis. She did not know what else she could do to persuade him that it was long since over; that her love for Lon had turned into disgust when she learned that he had married for money.

But any further thought of that would have to wait. Jack was right. She was more tired than she had suspected. She removed her clothes and partly unpacked her suitcase. Then she made some coffee, pulled on her new hoppi coat and sat down outside on the lanai.

White clouds moved with the trade winds against a deep blue sky. The air was fresh. White caps could be glimpsed on the ocean in the distance. And below, on the Ali Wai, a small one-man boat sailed on a starboard track.

Betty had enjoyed seeing Japan, but it was good to be back in Hawaii. Though she had lived here only a few months, it felt like home. A gradual relaxation came over her. After a peanut butter sandwich at noon, she decided to lie down for a while. That was the last she remembered until a voice woke her up.

"Hey! How long you been asleep?" It was Audrey. She came over to the bed and gave Betty a welcoming aloha kiss.

"Thanks for the greeting cards," said Betty, sitting up and rubbing her tousled blonde head. "What time is it?"

"Six o'clock. I was a bit late getting away from the office this afternoon. How was your trip?"

"Wonderful."

"Get up. I want to hear about it."

While Betty went to the bathroom and revived herself with a cold towel, Audrey made a pitcher of island punch and took it out onto the lanai. Betty pulled on her hoppi coat and joined her roommate a few moments later.

"Before I tell you about the trip, what's new at the office?" she asked, as a preliminary to bringing up the matter of Cheryl's call to Jack in Japan.

"Plenty," said the Chinese girl.

"Oh?" Betty looked at her quizzically.

"Iwalani has threatened to look for another public relations agency."

"But why?" Betty stared at Audrey, astounded at this information.

"Who knows? I've tried to pry it out of Warson, but he's not talking. I don't really know if he knows anything."

Betty thought that over in silence. She wondered if this could be another case of intrigue on the part of Cheryl Canton?

She even dared wonder if the brunette might be trying to force Jack's hand by making him choose between her or losing the account. A surge of resentment caused her face to grow a shade darker.

"Did Jack drop any hint about it on the trip?" Audrey asked. She had been pouring a drink and missed the subtle change in Betty's mood.

"If he knew about it, he didn't say anything. But how would he know?"

"He got a call — "

"Yes, I know," Betty snapped.

Audrey gave her a startled look. "But you just asked how would he know? What's wrong?"

"You're the only one I told out here about what happened to me back in St. Louis, Audrey. I should have been more careful who I trusted with that information."

"What the hell are you talking about?" Audrey put down her glass.

"Who else could have told Cheryl that I came to Hawaii on the rebound after an unfortunate love affair?"

Audrey looked as if she could not believe what she was hearing. Her dark, slant eyes narrowed.

"You think I did?"

"Well — did you?" Betty looked at her evenly.

"I ought to kick you out of this apartment for thinking that!" the Chinese girl exclaimed vehemently. "Of course I didn't! What do you think I am, a common gossip?"

It was Betty's turn to be startled. Audrey's anger did not seem like a cover up. Her words and mood had the ring of truth.

"I'm sorry if I've offended you, Audrey. I truly am," said Betty apologetically. But she was completely at a loss, now, to explain how Cheryl had found out about her.

"I think it's high time you do some explaining. You said you knew about Warson's call to Jack. Then you start talking about something else."

"Warson called Jack?" Betty knew instantly that something had gone on that she knew nothing about.

"Yes. He called him and told him that Iwalani was threatening to fire Benning & Associates."

277

"Jack told me that Cheryl had called."

"Maybe she did. I don't know. But I was right there when Warson called him."

"Hummmm," Betty muttered. "There must have been two calls."

"What's this about Cheryl?" asked Audrey.

"Jack told me she had called him and told him about that fellow I was involved with in St. Louis — that I was still carrying the torch."

"Cheryl isn't as smart as I thought," Audrey commented.

"If she wanted to upset Jack she certainly accomplished her purpose. He's been giving me the cold shoulder ever since," said Betty unhappily.

After a moment Audrey said. "Just what is your relationship with Jack? Those around the office have been wondering for some time. And that's not gossip. It's common knowledge that the two of you are attracted to each other."

"I wish I knew," Betty replied.

"Do you love him?"

"I — I don't know."

"Oh, brother! What does it take?

Someone to sit on you and pound some sense into your head? You keep on like this and I'm just the gal to do it." Suddenly she stood up. "Gotta get dressed. Gotta date. I'll hear about the trip later. Get some rest tonight and we'll see what gives at the office in the morning." Audrey disappeared into the apartment.

That night, as she lay awake in bed, Betty tried to figure out what could have happened. If Warson had called with the information about Iwalani it could account for some of Jack's behavior. He would naturally be upset about it. But his attitude toward Betty had to be the result of Cheryl's call. At least in part. Suddenly, she remembered that Jack had said Cheryl had told him that among other things. Among other things . . . ? What could that have been about, if not Iwalani?

All at once, Betty experienced a sinking feeling. Was Jack like Lon? Would he do what had to be done to hold on to the account? Marrying Cheryl would assure that. It might get him the whole company. She could not believe that of him. And yet, at one time she could not have believed it of Lon. She was beginning to question her wisdom when it came to men. Was she so gullible that anyone could take her in. She fell asleep wondering.

When Betty awoke the next morning, she felt rested from the trip though her mind was still troubled. Audrey had been up late and she was the one who dragged getting out of bed. Betty fixed breakfast for both of them.

"Next time you fix breakfast put a headache pill on the plate for me. My date last night was a drip," Audrey complained.

Betty laughed.

They arrived at the office shortly before nine o'clock. Jack and the two men were already there. Betty's desk was piled high with mail and memos. On top of all that she had the portfolio that now had to be typed into memo form and many extra copies run off. Jack wanted each member of the mission to have a copy. After all that she would go to work on his expense accounts from the trip.

She started on the mail that was addressed to Jack. A lot of it was routine. She separated the important ones and took them into him.

"Did you get rested last night?" he asked matter-of-factly.

"Yes. I feel better and ready to get back to work."

"There'll be plenty to do for the next few days." He did not elaborate.

Back at her desk, Betty began going through more mail. Warson had been handling the things that were addressed to Benning & Associates and he had made notes for Jack's information on what disposition had been made. All at once Betty came to an envelope addressed to Benning & Associates that had been resealed. Across the front of the envelope Warson had written 'opened by mistake.'

She took out the letter and was surprised to see that it started out 'Dear Betty . . . ' It was from Peg Waters and she had forgotten to put Betty's name on the envelope. Warson had opened it, inadvertently.

But as Betty read the letter, which was

merely a newsy friendly note, she began to look thoughtful. Then she frowned. In it, Peg had told her some more about Lon working for his wife's family, and had enclosed a clipping from the business page of the St. Louis newspaper saying that Lon had been given added duties. But the sentence that made Betty frown was this one.'So, Betty dear, if you still carry the torch for Lon Holderness (which I doubt after all this time with those good looking men in Hawaii) forget him. He was never worthy of your love and never worth all the heartbreak you went through.'

Betty put the letter down and stared into space, her mind racing. If Warson had read that — ? Suddenly she arose, picked up the letter and walked to Warson's desk.

"I see you opened this by mistake," she said.

Warson looked up from his work and nodded.

"Did you read it?"

"No." Warson quickly averted his eyes, but not before Betty saw a look of guilt in them.

Without another word she went back to her desk and sat down. So Warson was the one! It figured. He worked on the Iwalani account. He was Cheryl's listening post in the Benning Agency. No wonder the girl knew everything that was going on. Betty remembered how upset Warson had been when he found out that she and Jack had been out together shortly after her arrival on Oahu. That was one bit of information that he did not want to pass along to Cheryl. The man was not trustworthy, in any event. Betty wondered if she should tell Jack, but decided against it. She did not want to be the cause of any firing. But from this moment on she would be careful what she said or did around Warson Graham.

Jack said nothing to her or anyone else about the Iwalani situation that day or the next. Betty began to wonder if it was as bad as she had thought. It might have been just a lot of talk. But the following Monday was another matter. Jack spent that morning at Iwalani with Warson and when they came back to the office Jack looked grim. He left for lunch, saying that he would not be back that afternoon.

"If you need me for anything I'll be out at the Canton place," he told Betty.

Right away Betty knew why he was going. This whole business was beginning to fit into a pattern. Iwalani had threatened to hire another agency, at the behest of the owners of the company. If Jack was going to the Canton home, who else would he be seeing there but Cheryl? And if he was going to see Cheryl what else would it be about, if not to hang onto the account? Betty was at the end of her rope. She was tired of thinking.

"Have you got a date tonight?" she asked Audrey.

"Nope and glad of it. I need some rest for a change."

"Let's stop somewhere for dinner on the way home," Betty suggested. She wanted to keep her mind off Jack if she could. Knowing that he was with Cheryl this afternoon contributed nothing to her peace of mind.

"Good deal," said Audrey.

They closed the office at five o'clock and went in Audrey's car to Waikiki.

There they parked on Kuhio and went through the International Market to the Cock's Roost, a bar and restaurant that Audrey assured her was not a tourist place so much as it was frequented by the many people who worked in and around Waikiki.

"Hello, Pete," Audrey called out to the bartender as they went by on the way to the table.

"Hey, Audrey. How you been. Don't go to the table yet. Have a drink at the bar," he called back.

It was early and the place was not crowded. Audrey asked Betty if she minded. She didn't, so they sat on stools at the bar. Betty was introduced to Pete, a Chinaman who had known Audrey since she was a kid.

"My friend here," said Audrey, "works with me at Benning & Associates. She's Jack's secretary."

"Ah. You the girl that took Jane's place," Pete beamed.

Betty wondered how Pete knew about that. They ordered drinks and when Pete came back and set them before the girls he leaned his elbow on the bar.

"How's Jack? I don't see him much any more, since he's become successful."

"Funny but I had the notion that Jack was always successful," Betty replied. And she meant it. It was hard for her to think of him otherwise.

"Naw. When he first came out here it was touch and go. Once in awhile he'd come in here. And when his mother came out to see him they'd always come here. I knew her well before Jack ever came out here. She was in show business you know. A real charmer. But, anyway, after Jack got connected with the Canton family his business started picking up. Have another drink, girls?"

Betty didn't want another. She reflected on what the bartender had just said. The Canton family again. And that meant Cheryl. She wondered what was going on out there in the beautiful home in Kahala?

During dinner and the rest of the evening she refused to think about it. Every time she caught herself entertaining thoughts of Jack, she concentrated on clothes or the weather or music or anything she could focus on for minutes at a time. Such self-discipline paid off. Betty was able to get a good night's sleep.

It was a good thing she did. Jack came in that morning looking as if he had slept not at all. There was a harried look in his eyes. His face was drawn. Moreover, he was irritable. He barked at Betty and others in the office. Late that morning he called her in for dictation. Most of it was routine and none of it concerned Iwalani. In the middle of one of the letters he stopped, got up and began pacing the floor.

"What's the matter?" she asked, after she had watched him for a moment. She had never seen him quite this tense.

"Nothing," he replied, snapping at her. Then he stopped. "I'm sorry. Maybe I have been getting too worked up. I have another important meeting this afternoon."

"Then you had better calm down."

"Yes. I know." He sat down, but did not resume dictating.

"Would you like for me to leave? I can get started on the things you have already given me. You can finish this last letter later."

"No. Stay here. I'll get at it in a moment."

Betty waited. All at once, she remembered some advice Naoko Tsutomi had given her. She wondered if it would be forward of her if she helped Jack relax. Then, all at once, she quit thinking about herself. Forward of her or not, Jack needed help. Suddenly she got up and stood behind his chair.

"Maybe this will help you to calm down," she said. And with that she began massaging the muscles of his shoulders. He looked around at her, startled.

"What's with this?" he asked.

"I'm just trying to relax you for your meeting. Does this help?"

"Very much."

She kneaded his muscles with her hands and fingers, gently yet firmly. She had never massaged anyone before. The feel of his broad shoulders beneath her hands stirred powerful emotions in her. She fought to hold her own reactions down. The main thing was to help him, not to complicate things for herself. She thought she felt him relaxing under her ministrations. She kept it up a while longer.

"There. Did that feel good? Do you feel better?" She sat down and picked up her steno pad.

Jack looked at her for a long moment. Slowly he smiled. His eyes grew soft as he gazed into hers.

"That was wonderful. Thanks."

"*Doo itashimashita*," 'it was nothing,' she replied using Japanese, only because she had been thinking of Naoko and what she had just done to help Jack.

"What do you mean it was nothing? It was great."

"The Japanese words just came to me. I guess I'm still thinking of our wonderful trip," said Betty.

"Let's finish that letter," said Jack with resolve. "Then I'm off to another meeting."

He finished the letter, told Betty he would be at Iwalani through the lunch hour and possibly on into the afternoon. He said for her to call him if anything important came up.

Early that afternoon the telephone rang

and Betty answered it. It was the cable office calling. A cable for Mr. Benning had just been received. They would like to read it over the phone and send the confirming copy over later.

"Mr. Benning is not in. Maybe you had better just send it over."

"It's marked urgent. Couldn't you take it down? Maybe you could reach him with the message. It'll take us awhile to deliver the copy."

"Very well," said Betty reaching for her note pad. "Who is it from?"

"It's from a Helen Bader in New Zealand," said the girl at the other end.

14

ANY vestiges of hope that things might work out for her began disappearing as the girl in the cable office read Betty the message. Through the turmoil that was growing in her mind, she fought to get the words down in shorthand. It was over in ten seconds, for the cable contained less than two dozen words. She stared at her notes, wondering why her aspirations seemed forever doomed by a relentless fate.

"Do you wish to read it back to me?" came the girl's voice.

"Yes, I'd better," Betty sighed. She started reading. "Will arrive Hono Airport, New Flt. 211 at 1700 Hours. Meet me with wheel chair. Ankle broken in ski accident. Love. Helen."

"That is correct," said the girl. "I'll put a copy in the mail to you right away."

Betty typed the message, then sat there looking at it for a moment. If this was bad news for her it might be equally bad for Cheryl Canton. There was little consolation for Betty in that, but at least she was not alone. She took hold of herself. Jack told her to call him if anything urgent came up. This looked pretty urgent to Betty. Helen Bader would be arriving in less than three hours.

Betty picked up the phone and called Iwalani. Jack was not there. He and some others had gone to lunch and had not returned. Betty left a message for him to call. And she asked that he be told that it was urgent. It was close to three o'clock before she heard from him.

"I hope what you have is really urgent," he said immediately, "because I'm terribly busy."

She read him the message in a non-committal tone.

"What next," he groaned. "I can't possibly meet that plane. Let me talk to Billy."

"You sent Billy to Maui to get information for the Land and Development Company's quarterly report. Remember?" said Betty. "And Warson is supposed to be with you."

"Yes, yes," he said impatiently. "Give me time to think."

Betty waited.

"I'm going to ask you to do me a favor," he said in a moment. "You'll have to meet the plane for me. Get Audrey to help if you need to. You can close the office early. Will you do that for me?

"Oh, one other thing. Take Helen to my apartment, rather than to a hotel. She might already have a reservation at the Kahala Hilton, but take her to my apartment anyway. If she's got a broken ankle I can't be running out to Kahala all the time, looking after her. And remind her that I told her to stay off of those damned skis."

"Yes, sir," said Betty. If she hadn't been put down already, she certainly was now.

When they hung up, she walked over to Audrey's desk and showed her the message. Audrey read it and looked up, an amused smile curling her lips.

"Too bad it ain't her neck that was broken instead of an ankle," said the Chinese girl.

"Jack can't meet her. He asked me to do it for him."

"That's crust, I must admit." Audrey looked at her sympathetically.

"Would you help?" Betty inquired. "Jack said for me to ask you, if I thought I needed help. And I think I do."

"Sure, kid, but who's to look after the office?"

"He said to close early."

"He's the boss."

At four o'clock that afternoon Betty and Audrey headed for the airport in Audrey's car. They parked and went into the terminal building and located a New Zealand Air office. Betty explained to the man in charge that they needed a wheel chair for the person who was arriving.

"Yes. I know about that. The captain of the flight radioed us. We will take the passenger off ahead of the others. If you care to wait here you can accompany us out to the plane when it arrives. It should be making its approach very shortly," said the man courteously.

Betty and Audrey sat down.

"Should we buy her a lei with some

thorns in it?" Audrey wondered.

Betty chuckled. "I'd love to."

"Come with me, please," said the man a few moments later.

The girls followed him out to one of the international arrival gates where an attendant was waiting with a wheel chair. The plane was already on the ground and was making its way to the ramp.

"Who is this person?" asked the man. "The captain in radioing asked for VIP treatment."

"Her name is Helen Bader," said Betty. "I don't know anything more than that."

The plane pulled up to the unloading ramp and the engines were turned off. In a moment, the man took the wheel chair from the attendant and told Betty and Audrey to follow him onto the plane, where somewhat of a commotion was in progress in the first class section.

"Sign right there, Captain," came a girl's loud voice.

Betty looked and saw Helen Bader, her leg propped up over the arm of a seat. The Captain of the aircraft was signing his name to the cast that was enclosed around her broken ankle. The two were surrounded by hostesses and another officer. All were smiling.

"Aha! This will be known as Helen's all star cast!" the blonde exclaimed and everyone broke into laughter.

The man who had accompanied Betty and Audrey to the plane moved forward with the wheel chair. Helen Bader was lifted by no less a personage than the Captain, with an assist by the Navigator, who placed her in the wheel chair.

"Thanks boys, and good luck." She threw kisses to them and the hostesses and everyone else she could see.

"I'm Betty Lane, Mr. Benning's secretary," said Betty, moving to the girl's side. "You may not remember me, but we met at his office. And this is Audrey Ching. She also works there."

Helen Bader smiled at the two girls, then nodded. "Of course I remember. How have you been?"

"Jack is tied up and he asked us to meet you," Betty explained, ignoring Helen Bader's inquiry. She was a bit shocked at Helen Bader's appearance. She looked older than she had only a few short months ago in the Benning Agency. Betty decided she may have suffered some pain from the broken ankle.

"How sweet of you to come, but how mean of him not to," said the blonde.

At that moment the man pushed the wheel chair toward the entrance. Farewells were called by the cabin personnel. Helen Bader waved back as she was wheeled into the terminal building. She was provided further VIP treatment when the man announced that her luggage would be delivered, without going through customs, to her transportation wherever it might be.

"I'll get my car and bring it around," said Audrey and hurried off.

"Is all my luggage here? Good grief," Helen Bader explained to Betty, "when I broke my ankle I was up on Mt. Cook. They flew me to Christchurch and left all my things at the Hermitage. I still haven't seen them. My clothes, my cosmetics, my makeup. I feel a mess and I guess I look like one too. Thank goodness, Jack couldn't meet me. I wouldn't want him to see me like this."

"He said he warned you not to go skiing," said Betty.

"He did, and I know he must be furious with me for breaking my ankle," said the blonde smiling helplessly.

At the pick-up curb they waited for Audrey to drive up in her car. Meanwhile, attendants had secured Helen Bader's luggage and brought it to them.

"My crutches! I left them on the plane! Oh dear, can we send someone back for them?"

That proved unnecessary for at that moment one of the hostesses from the flight ran up to them, carrying the crutches. She beamed at Helen Bader.

"We wouldn't let you get away without them," she said.

"What a darling you are!" Helen Bader looked up at Betty. "Isn't it wonderful how helpful all the airline people are?" She looked back at the hostess. "Thank you, my dear. Thanks a million."

It occurred to Betty that she was seeing a side to Helen Bader that she had not recognized before. It was a maturity that seemed somewhat older than her appearance. She was still puzzling over her thoughts when Audrey drove up.

Getting all the luggage and Helen Bader into the car was a major undertaking, but they were assisted by the office manager of New Zealand Air, two porters and the hostess who had remained to help, if needed. Finally they were ready to go. Helen Bader waved a crutch out of the window.

"Next time I see you, these will be kindling," she gave a hearty laugh as Audrey drove off, leaving the airline personnel waving their goodbyes. She spoke to Betty then, "Did Jack get a hotel reservation, my dear?"

"He said to take you to his apartment."

"What?" Helen Bader exclaimed.

"He said he wouldn't have time to look after you, if he had to run out to Kahala."

"He doesn't have to look after me. I'm quite capable of looking after myself!" she declared, indignantly.

"Those were my instructions," said Betty, wondering all the more about the girl. She didn't sound like someone who was having an affair with Jack.

"Very well," the blonde agreed. "I

won't argue the point with you. That's a score I'll have to settle with Jack. By the way, when did he say he'd be home?"

"He didn't."

"He's really terribly busy, isn't he?" Helen Bader mused.

"Yes, terribly," Betty agreed, wondering, at the same time, how he was doing with Iwalani. The outcome of today's meeting would tell her a lot about him. Was he another Lon Holderness? Or was he the man she had hoped he was?

"Tell me something, girls," Helen Bader spoke up as they drove through Honolulu, "is there a little restaurant in the International Market by the name of the Cock's Roost? Is that still there?"

"Why, yes," Audrey spoke up. "Betty and I were just there yesterday."

"Is Pete, the bartender, still there?"

"Yes." Audrey and Betty turned to each other at the same instant. Audrey almost ran into the curb, she was so surprised.

"Could we stop in for cocktails?" Helen asked. "I'd love to say hello to Pete. I think I can make it in there and up those steps on my crutches and I'd love to have a visit with you two girls. You can fill me in a lot about Jack."

"Are you Jack's — ?" Betty cried.

"I can't believe it!" said Audrey.

"What are you kids talking about?" asked the blonde.

"Pete told us yesterday that Jack and his mother used to come in there — " Betty said.

"Why, of course we did. I've known Pete longer even than Jack has."

"You can't be old enough to be his mother!" Audrey exclaimed.

Helen Bader preened herself. "Well, I've tried hard to keep my looks and my figure over the years. You have to do that in show business, you know. After Jack's father died I worked harder than ever. Then I married Mike Bader, but that didn't last long. Jack and he never did hit it off."

One great weight was suddenly lifted from Betty's mind. Where once she glumly contemplated his visits to Portland, she now considered this person he visited with something akin to affection. She saw a lot of this remarkable woman in Jack. He had much of her charm when he took a notion to exercise it. He could command attention when he spoke. But she knew, too, with womanly instinct that he could still learn a lot from the maternal side of his parents. She was great! And that was putting it mildly.

Helen and Pete had a loud and happy reunion when they reached the Cock's Roost. Helen was pleased that Betty and Audrey could take some time for a drink and visit. She plied them both with questions about Jack. She had been fearful for some time that he had been working too hard, that he was to tense.

"I'm depending on you two girls to help me with him," she concluded, "especially you, Betty, since you're his secretary."

Betty toyed with the notion of telling her about the massage she had given him, but decided against it. Then abruptly Helen decided she should move on. "Drop me off at his apartment then you two go on. I'm sure you have things to do this evening."

They did not drop her off. Instead they helped her in, saw to it that one of the maintenance men delivered her luggage, then went back to Audrey's car, which had been parked in a nearby garage.

"Well, will miracles never cease!" Audrey observed as they drove home. "Whoever would have guessed it?"

"I surely wouldn't have," Betty admitted. But then, she had never guessed that she would be out here in Hawaii or meet a man like Jack. Was it possible that another miracle might happen? In any event there was no way she could find out until the morning when she would hear what had transpired at Iwalani.

But that information was not forthcoming at the office next morning. Jack came in looking tired and wan. He thanked Betty and Audrey for being of so much help to Helen then went into his office and closed the door. Later that morning he called Betty in and dictated two unimportant letters. He glanced at his wrist watch. It was coming on noon.

"I've got another meeting starting most any time now. And after that I may be gone for the rest of the day, trying to get Helen settled for awhile until her ankle knits. I might have to talk with you later on. Have you any plans for later this afternoon or evening?" he asked.

"No," said Betty.

"If I don't phone you here at the office, I might try to reach you at your apartment." His tone was somber.

"I'll be there," she said.

Just as Betty was leaving his office to return to her desk, Cheryl swept in. She and Betty almost collided. The brunette glared at her for being in the way. Betty was about to step aside in deference but then she thought, damned if she would! It was Cheryl who finally went around. Betty left the office, closing the door behind her.

Audrey, Billy and Warson were all glancing toward her and the closed door. Betty noticed it and smiled toward them. At least she had achieved one triumph over Cheryl Canton. From now on she could hold her head high, no matter what happened.

She heard voices in the private office but could not distinguish words. Cheryl's voice was heated, Jack's quiet but firm. Betty took out envelopes and paper and began typing the letters Jack had dictated. It was much better use of her time rather than trying to eavesdrop. But she found herself growing tense when, during a lull in her typing, she distinctly heard Cheryl mention her name during a heated exchange.

So, she was the subject of the meeting. That really didn't surprise her. Instinctively she had known for some time that Cheryl was trying to torpedo her. She wondered if Jack would sacrifice her to save the Iwalani account? Then suddenly the door to Jack's office swung open.

Cheryl Canton came out. A satisfied smile was on her lips. She looked down at Betty in passing. There was no mistaking her attitude. Betty's heart sank. Cheryl looked like a person who had gotten her way; like a person who always got her way sooner or later. Then she disappeared into the corridor.

Jack left ten minutes later, saying nothing to anyone.

A terrible hopelessness came over Betty. She fought back tears, feeling the compassionate glances of her fellow workers from time to time. But somehow she managed to make it through the rest of the day without showing her true emotions. Audrey was to meet a friend for early dinner so Betty went to the apartment alone. She was surprised when Jack called around six o'clock. She hadn't really expected it of him.

"Can you come to my apartment?" he asked.

"Why, yes. I can, if that's what you'd like me to do."

"Please."

"Now?"

"Yes."

"So?"

"I'm going to fire you." He was calm, even solicitous and his voice was gentle.

A great bitterness swept through her. What was life all about anyway? Other girls fell in love, were loved in return, married, had children — achieved normal happiness. Twice the wizard curtains had opened for her, revealing a bright and promising life ahead. And twice they had been cruelly jerked shut, condemning her to hopeless rejection. Love go away. Let her alone. Get lost. She turned to leave.

"Wait," said Jack.

"Why?" She gave him a look of disillusionment and disgust.

"Because I've got another job lined up for you."

"Never mind. I can look after myself."

"That's where you're wrong. You need someone to watch over you every minute of the day."

"Coming from you that's a real gasser," Betty shot back.

She wanted out of there, but Jack grabbed her and whirled her around. She struggled as his arms slipped around her. She beat at him with her fists. When she attempted to kick him he lifted her off of her feet. Jack smiled down at her.

"You'll listen to me if I have to hold you all night."

"I want no part of you. Let me go," she begged.

"Never."

Hearing him use that word caused her to look up. She was mystified by the soft look in his eyes and the smile on his lips.

"Long before Cheryl brought the matter up, I had determined to have you change jobs," he said.

"You're doing what she wants done. Lots of luck with her and your precious Iwalani account." There was contempt in her voice.

"Cheryl is in for a shock. She doesn't know about the other job I have in mind for you. When she finds out, Iwalani may or may not be my account. And, frankly, I don't care. That much she does know."

"Let me go. You're talking crazy."

"Is wanting to marry you crazy?" he asked.

Betty wondered if she had heard right. She looked up at him in disbelief. Either her ears had deceived her, or he was pulling another cruel hoax at her expense. But, as she searched his eyes, she suddenly saw something in them that she had overlooked. They were filled with love and longing for her.

"I love you," he murmured.

"Oh, Jack, I love you too, so very much," she cried.

All of a sudden he let her go.

"We've got to hurry," he said. "Helen will be waiting at the hair dresser's. I told her that I was going to introduce her to her new daughter-in-law tonight, so she's going all out for you."

Betty could think of nothing to say. She just kept looking up at Jack adoringly. She did not hear the haunting tone of a conch shell coming from a catamaran or the sounds of late afternoon traffic drifting up from Kalakaua. The lowering sun began tinting surf and sky with rainbow hues, but she saw only Jack. She clung to him, knowing that, finally, she had found the one man she would love for the rest of her life.

THE END

Other titles in the
Ulverscroft Large Print Series:

TO FIGHT THE WILD
Rod Ansell and Rachel Percy

Lost in uncharted Australian bush, Rod Ansell survived by hunting and trapping wild animals, improvising shelter and using all the bushman's skills he knew.

COROMANDEL
Pat Barr

India in the 1830s is a hot, uncomfortable place, where the East India Company still rules. Amelia and her new husband find themselves caught up in the animosities which seethe between the old order and the new.

THE SMALL PARTY
Lillian Beckwith

A frightening journey to safety begins for Ruth and her small party as their island is caught up in the dangers of armed insurrection.

THE WILDERNESS WALK
Sheila Bishop

Stifling unpleasant memories of a misbegotten romance in Cleave with Lord Francis Aubrey, Lavinia goes on holiday there with her sister. The two women are thrust into a romantic intrigue involving none other than Lord Francis.

THE RELUCTANT GUEST
Rosalind Brett

Ann Calvert went to spend a month on a South African farm with Theo Borland and his sister. They both proved to be different from her first idea of them, and there was Storr Peterson — the most disturbing man she had ever met.

ONE ENCHANTED SUMMER
Anne Tedlock Brooks

A tale of mystery and romance and a girl who found both during one enchanted summer.

CLOUD OVER MALVERTON
Nancy Buckingham

Dulcie soon realises that something is seriously wrong at Malverton, and when violence strikes she is horrified to find herself under suspicion of murder.

AFTER THOUGHTS
Max Bygraves

The Cockney entertainer tells stories of his East End childhood, of his RAF days, and his post-war showbusiness successes and friendships with fellow comedians.

MOONLIGHT AND MARCH ROSES
D. Y. Cameron

Lynn's search to trace a missing girl takes her to Spain, where she meets Clive Hendon. While untangling the situation, she untangles her emotions and decides on her own future.

NURSE ALICE IN LOVE
Theresa Charles

Accepting the post of nurse to little Fernie Sherrod, Alice Everton could not guess at the romance, suspense and danger which lay ahead at the Sherrod's isolated estate.

POIROT INVESTIGATES
Agatha Christie

Two things bind these eleven stories together — the brilliance and uncanny skill of the diminutive Belgian detective, and the stupidity of his Watson-like partner, Captain Hastings.

LET LOOSE THE TIGERS
Josephine Cox

Queenie promised to find the long-lost son of the frail, elderly murderess, Hannah Jason. But her enquiries threatened to unlock the cage where crucial secrets had long been held captive.

THE TWILIGHT MAN
Frank Gruber

Jim Rand lives alone in the California desert awaiting death. Into his hermit existence comes a teenage girl who blows both his past and his brief future wide open.

DOG IN THE DARK
Gerald Hammond

Jim Cunningham breeds and trains gun dogs, and his antagonism towards the devotees of show spaniels earns him many enemies. So when one of them is found murdered, the police are on his doorstep within hours.

THE RED KNIGHT
Geoffrey Moxon

When he finds himself a pawn on the chessboard of international espionage with his family in constant danger, Guy Trent becomes embroiled in moves and countermoves which may mean life or death for Western scientists.